ROMANCE IN PROVENCE

MARIE LEROUGE

MLR

Published by MLR Paris
ISBN 978-2-9567945-8-5

Cover design by Lydie Wallon @2LI
First published in France by Amorosa in February 2018
Original title: *L'héritière comblée*
Translated by Sheila Macbrayne

Contents

CHAPTER 1

Thirty-something blues

Paris, July 4th 2015

The large newspaper office hummed with activity. Mathilde reread her article, eyes glued to the computer screen. Every evening, to meet the press deadline, she cut herself off from her surroundings. All that mattered was the text in front of her. Her slender fingers flitted over the keyboard, adding final corrections to her article destined for the Society page in the Paris paper the next morning.

Opposite her, their screens back to back, Benoît sat watching her in wry amusement, waiting for her to look up with a triumphant smile. For the last three years their desks had faced each other, and he had learned to predict all her reactions.

Mathilde duly relaxed, gazed over at her colleague, batted her eyelashes at him and breathed a sigh of relief.

"Done! I've forwarded it to you to check."

"Let's pop out for a drink first!"

"Sure, but on one condition, and you know what that is."

Benoît shrugged.

"OK, I won't mention today's date, I promise, though I can't see why you obstinately refuse...."

"Benoît – one more word and I'll..."

"I mean obstinately refuse to let us wish you a happy birthday! If you were getting on for forty like me I'd understand, but you are only THIRTY, a woman in her prime..."

Mathilde seized the first file to hand and brandished it at him threateningly. Benoît pretended to shield his face.

"No, not the *Urban Youth* file, PLEASE! It weighs a ton, and your aim is useless. Put it down at once. All right, I'm sorry - I'll shut up."

She duly put it down.

"Now you've calmed down, shall we go?"

Benoît came round to her side of the desk, took her by the elbow and escorted her out.

They moved smartly through the long glass-walled office, past colleagues hunched over their screens and went into the lift. They fooled around with the revolving doors in the lobby and emerged onto the pavement.

Benoît opened a packet of cigarettes which Mathilde promptly snatched away.

"Give that back! You know perfectly well I can't write without my daily dose of nicotine."

"No way! You have a heart condition and a twelve year-old son who you adore and who adores you."

"OK, I promise I'll give up if that's what you want. In the meantime, will you let me smoke a final cigarette? Please Mattie, hand it over."

"No! I don't want to lose my best friend."

"You're somewhat morose today, my dear."

Arm in arm, they headed for their usual café. On spotting them the owner promptly produced two glasses filled with champagne. Benoît handed one to Mathilde, cupping his hand over her mouth to stop her protesting.

"It's on me," said the café owner "I have just heard of the arrival of my first grandson!"

Mathilde looked content and the two men exchanged a look of complicity.

"What's his name?" she asked.

"Théo."

She made a toast: "To Théo!"

They clinked their glasses. Benoît watched her sip her drink, looking relaxed for once.

"I'm pleased the *Urban Youth* article is done and dusted. We made a good job of it, didn't we?"

"True – the two of us make a great team. Unfortunately..."

She flinched. He hesitated, then rushed on:

"I'd have preferred to wait till tomorrow to tell you this, but you know how quickly news spreads round the office. I wanted to be the first to tell you."

"Go on, I'm listening".

"I've been appointed Editor-in-chief of the online publication."

She laid her hand over his.

"That's great news. I'm really touched to be the first to know. Congratulations my friend, I'm really pleased for you. You deserve it. You are the best."

He noticed that she had tears in her eyes.

"And your promotion has come just at the right moment," she added, finishing her drink, "I'm getting a bit tired of feeling your adoring gaze on me when I'm working. I need a change myself."

She got off her stool and embraced him.

"Damn it, I'm crying. This has to happen today of all days. I'll miss you, you rat."

He stroked her hair.

"I'm not going far. You'll be able to see me from your desk."

She pulled back.

"Who will I be working for then?"

"My replacement writes well and she's not bad looking."

"You mean it's a WOMAN?!"

She looked ruffled.

"I was joking. I am irreplaceable. My appointment will be announced during the editorial meeting tomorrow morning. I can't tell you any more at this stage."

He glanced at this watch.

"We've chatted enough. Let's get back to work."

They took leave of the café owner and returned to the newspaper office in silence.

"I've got an odd premonition," said Mathilde in the lift.

"Don't worry. I was silly, sorry. I shouldn't have brought this up today."

"It's not that. I feel as if my life is about to change."

"Because you have reached a milestone?"

"Don't start that again!"

She hesitated for an instant.

"No, because I want it to change."

The lift doors slid open. She stepped out first.

"Are you doing anything special this evening?" he muttered, planting a little kiss on her ear lobe.

"I'm having a few girlfriends round."

"Pity. I've discovered this new Lebanese restaurant nearby. I was hoping to take you there."

"You're a darling but they'd be disappointed. If I've understood correctly they've laid on some kind of surprise."

"I thought you hated surprises."

"It depends."

Back at their desks he noticed that she had put on what he called her brave little soldier expression.

"Are you OK?"

"Everything's hunky-dory," she grinned, "I'm thirty years old, I don't have a boyfriend, my biological clock is ticking and I feel pathetic."

Just then the desk phone started to ring. She answered it while Benoît pretended to be absorbed in his work.

"The Managing Editor wants to see me. I wonder why."

On her return, she threw herself into her seat, looking faintly irritated.

"Well?" he asked without looking up.

"He liked our report. He found the approach interesting, the interviews compelling and the conclusion interesting."

“That was all?!”

“Then he told me it’s me who’s replacing you. Apparently it was your idea.”

Her tone was cold and furious. Benoît flushed and wiped his brow.

“He already had you in mind.”

“The bottom line,” she went on, “is that I am promoted to manage the department but with no pay rise and nobody to replace me. It’s a case of take it or leave it. I get the job title but not the salary that goes with it – it’s ridiculous. Not to mention the extra workload.”

Benoît frowned.

“I thought you’d react more positively. What more do you want?”

“A salary on a par with yours for a start. You know something - it’s not the money, it’s the principle. On top of that, I don’t have the right Boss Mindset and no desire whatsoever to run a department. All I want is the time to do serious investigative research and produce good articles.”

“There are times I don’t understand you Mattie. You throw me, you upset me, you disappoint me.”

“But it’s easy to understand! I’d have liked to continue working with you and for you, that’s all. I’m sick of being passed over, can’t you see?”

"Don't mix up your professional and private life. The guys who have dumped you got it wrong. You know I will never let you down, either inside or outside the office. OK, now it's out I might as well tell all. It's Odile who is to become my assistant. It was up to me to decide, but the job wouldn't have been right for you. It is impersonal and not very gratifying. You need to see your signature on your work. You need to touch, to feel what you are producing. You are the sensual type, sweetheart. Virtual is not for the likes of you."

Mathilde was furious.

"Odile, for God's sake - that's the last straw! You can bet that if she's there I won't set foot inside your office!"

"It's a shame you two started off so badly when you joined the team."

"Be honest, she set out to make things difficult for me."

"She has an excuse, she had family issues."

"Is that so?! I thought one shouldn't mix one's professional and private life!"

"You sure hold a grudge, which is a pity. Anyway, time is moving on. I'm still your boss and I give you permission to go and join your girlfriends. Have a nice evening, my darling. See you tomorrow morning."

Mathilde angrily grabbed her bag and left without saying goodbye.

Benoît waited a while, then went out to get cigarettes from the local shop. He regretted having been so direct. Would he have tread more carefully if she had accepted his dinner invitation? Not for the first time he wondered about Mathilde. She seemed pretty down – he really should try to be more sensitive.

CHAPTER 2

Romantic Montmartre

By the time Mathilde emerged from the Notre-Dame-de-Lorette metro station, she regretted having lost her temper. She had been unfair to Benoît. He was disappointed and had shown his feelings for once.

I always disappoint men, it's the way I am, she sighed.

She walked quickly up the *Rue des Martyrs*. This bustling Paris street was colourful during the day but quietened down as soon as the shops shut. The warm, early summer weather heralded a long fine evening, perfect for romance.

She followed a young couple walking hand in hand. Halfway up the street they stopped to admire the white shape of the *Sacré-Cœur* basilica appearing on the horizon. Mathilde came to an abrupt halt. They embraced. She suddenly saw herself in Christophe's arms in exactly the same spot, equally entranced by the romance of their city, although it had gradually lost its charm for her after he left her six months earlier.

One cold January evening on returning home from work she found a message on the kitchen table. The words, scribbled on the back of a crumpled envelope, stabbed her to the quick and still resounded in her head: *I don't feel happy with you. I'm leaving.*

It obsessed her. *He left me in such a cowardly fashion, just when I needed him most, after my father died so suddenly.* She relived that terrible evening when, overcome by rage, she had rushed out into the snowy streets searching blindly for him, realising that despite two years together she knew nothing about him. Shortly afterwards, Benoît, answering her desperate call, had joined her in a café in Pigalle and found her shaking with the cold and incapable of going back to her empty apartment.

The couple in the street set off again, with Mathilde in their wake. Since that evening in January, Christophe had given no sign of life and she had made no attempt to see him again. Gradually resignation took over from revolt, and she felt she was slowly healing, although it was still painful.

The *concierge* was looking out for her at the entrance to her apartment. As well as a pile of letters and cards she handed Mathilde a lavish bouquet of multicoloured roses. Her heart leapt. She hurriedly read the attached card. *'Congratulations on your promotion, with my everlasting and undying affection, Benoît'*.

No sooner inside her apartment, she tossed the pile of mail onto her desk and deposited the flowers on the kitchen table. Her answering machine had no messages. Holding back tears she went to run herself a bath.

In her bathroom mirror she saw a tall blond woman with pale blue eyes and a wan expression. She added lipstick and blusher. The illusion would not last long, she knew, but she was ready to face her friends.

The apartment filled with the cheerful chatter of Claire, Léa and Julie. Claire produced a bottle of chilled champagne. She had the cork out even before reaching the kitchen. She took the first glasses she could lay her hands on and filled them to the brim. Standing round the table they drank to their friendship. The first sip warmed Mathilde's heart. *Nothing can beat female bonding*. She felt grateful to her old schoolfriends for forcing her hand. Without them she would have spent the evening alone feeling sorry for herself.

Léa spotted the abandoned bouquet.

"Who is behind this thoughtful gesture?"

"Benoît," replied Mathilde unenthusiastically, "to make amends."

"He's adorable anyway," giggled Julie, "I've often wondered why you don't hook up with him. I'm sure he'd love to..."

"For a start he's ten years older than me, and I should remind you he's my boss! Actually, not for much longer. I was meaning to tell you - he's been promoted and I'm meant to step into his shoes, lucky me."

Shrill shrieks greeted the news. They clinked their glasses a second time.

"Getting to head a Department by the age of thirty is not bad going!" remarked Léa who worked for a women's magazine.

"It's a small department," Mathilde pointed out.

"Don't be so modest," said Claire, "We all know you're cut out for a brilliant career!"

"It's no big deal. I feel less and less ambitious. Does a successful career fulfil a woman's life?"

Julie put a comforting arm round her.

"No, darling, there's no shame in aiming for a great job with a great salary AND a Prince Charming, plus all the kids that come with it. Out of us all, only Claire is well placed to achieve all that. But we will get there eventually too, and you won't be last, I promise you. So dry your lovely eyes!"

Mathilde laughed through her tears. Léa produced some make-up from her bag and touched up her friend's face. Then the doorbell rang.

"I'll go!" shouted Julie a trifle hastily.

Mathilde stumbled after her. The figure of a man appeared in the doorway. It wasn't Christophe (who she still vainly hoped it might be). He did not look more than twenty-five. He was holding a pile of boxes from a deli in the *Rue des Martyrs* and an icebox full of bottles. Julie ushered him into the kitchen, dismissed the other three and shut the door. Meanwhile Claire and Léa directed Mathilde towards the lounge and onto the sofa. She looked at them inquiringly, but they merely smiled somewhat ruefully.

"What are you all up to?"

"This is your surprise!" announced Julie pointing to the young man who followed her in with a tray of glasses and plates piled with canapés.

It took Mathilde a couple of seconds to realise that the waiter was naked under his long apron, revealing muscular shoulders and nice strong legs. When he headed back to the kitchen after putting the tray on the coffee table, she was startled to spot a pair of nice firm buttocks. Spellbound, she barely heard her friends in a fit of giggles. Then she retorted:

"I must admit you've excelled yourselves. He's gorgeous, with a perfect physique and great looking skin. Where did you find this hunk?! Whose brainwave was this? Let me guess.... Claire? No, you are too proper. I'd say it's probably Julie. You were always the naughty one at school. Or maybe it's Léa, with all the things you encounter in the fashion business. Frankly, it's a really cool present, it must have cost you a bomb. A big thank you, girls!"

She got up from the sofa and gave each of them a grateful kiss.

"We didn't know what to give you," ventured Claire, 'And because we thought..."

"I see - you thought your friend Mattie was a bit depressed, so a handsome guy would be a great present for her thirtieth birthday. By the way where's he got to? Waiter, we're thirsty!" she shouted.

"Mattie, he might hear you!" muttered Julie.

"So? He's a waiter, isn't he?!"

"Yes, but..."

"See - I just need to call and he appears! Young man, some red wine please!"

She held out her glass. He bent over to serve her with deliberate slowness, giving her time to admire his powerful torso under the apron, and further down too, if she felt so inclined. He did not seem at all embarrassed.

"I haven't eaten a thing since this morning, I'm starving!" said Mathilde, "Aren't you lot?"

The waiter finished filling their glasses and returned to the kitchen. Lasciviously, she whispered:

"Can we keep him until the dessert? I've been deprived of dessert for months now. I'm getting desperate!"

"It's good to see you all worked up," smiled Léa, "your cheeks have gone quite pink, exactly as we were hoping. You can ask *dreamboat* to do overtime if you want. It's all paid for."

Mathilde hurled a cushion at her. When the waiter reappeared, fully dressed, with more food he found the four girls stretched out on the sofa howling with laughter, feathers still floating in the air.

Around midnight, with the excuse of relieving the babysitter, Claire signalled it was time to go. In the hall she said to Mathilde.

"You're feeling better, I can tell."

"Yes, I think I'm making progress. I haven't thought of Christophe once since the start of the evening."

"You are ready for a new relationship and it will be the right one, I promise you, *honey*."

They kissed each other goodbye.

Léa and Julie left next. On shutting the door, Mathilde paused in the hall and heard the clatter of dishes in the kitchen. She returned to the sofa and waited. *Dreamboat* didn't take long to join her, wearing close-fitting jeans and an open-necked white shirt. He placed two glasses and a champagne bucket on the coffee table, with a new bottle chilling inside.

"May I sit down?"

"Please do."

He settled down opposite her.

"I haven't introduced myself. My name is Hubert."

She smothered a giggle.

"And you are Mathilde, right?"

She burst out gaily: "You know everything!"

"It's a nice name. It suits you."

"My mother was reading *The Red and the Black* when she was expecting me."

"Mathilde de la Mole – an interesting character. Passionate. Your mother has good taste."

Surprised, Mathilde's manner softened. She had used what she called her *Stendhal Test* to gauge the level of culture of people who asked her about her first name.

"Would you like some champagne?" asked Hubert politely, as he had done all evening.

"Am I to assume you are still on duty?"

"Yes and no. It's up to you. We can stay here getting to know each other, or we could round off the evening in a club, unless your overwhelming fatigue means I should just tiptoe away."

"I haven't made up my mind yet. Let's just get to know each other as you suggest."

He filled her glass and handed it to her. She was surprised to see he took a mere sip of his.

"Don't you drink?!"

"Very little. I try to lead a healthy life. I'm the sporty sort."

"It shows!"

He smiled.

"Bodybuilding is different. Let's say my job requires having a certain physique."

"I understand. It must be a difficult job."

"It depends on the customer. Some are nicer than others. But generally speaking, it's fine."

"Why do you do it?"

He smiled teasingly:

"Ah, so you want me to tell you my life story! It's usually the other way round - the women I escort adore talking about themselves. But if you insist, I'll tell you. During office hours I work in IT, but I'm hyperactive and insomniac and thought I might take on a second job to supplement my income. It now pays more than my main job, but I haven't given it up because I'm lucid about it all –this other life will not last forever."

"You are extremely wise for one so young."

"Would you like to dance?"

"Why not, but my CD collection is pretty limited."

Hubert rummaged through her collection and produced an album of Abba's greatest hits which he inserted into the player on the bookshelf.

"It's not my sort of music but it'll do. Coming?"

Intrigued, Mathilde stood up, feeling slightly dizzy. Hubert's strong arms would stop her falling, she felt. The evening was taking an unexpected turn.

The young man gathered her into his arms to the opening bars of *Dancing Queen*. He improvised a syncopated *pas de deux* and she followed suit.

"You have a good sense of rhythm. Hold on, off we go...."

They speeded up. Mathilde felt elated. Her partner seemed to enjoy executing more and more complicated dance steps, but she managed to follow perfectly. When he began to pull her closer she pushed him away.

"I'm so thirsty!" she announced, flopping onto the sofa.

He went off to the kitchen to fetch her a glass of water and handed it to her with a smile.

"Apart from Francesca you are the only one who has been able to keep up with me at the first time of asking."

"Who is Francesca?" asked Mathilde, burning with curiosity.

"My partner, in a sense, or should I say a very beautiful woman who shares her life with me when it suits her. Totally free of charge, naturally."

"Do you love her?"

"I'm crazy about her. She's the sexiest woman in the world."

"Is she Italian?"

"She's half Venetian."

"What does she do in life?"

"She flies private jets for super rich businessmen."

"Impressive! How did you meet her? Tell me all!"

"Two years ago her girlfriends organised a party for her. I'd just started my new job. That evening she invited me to stay the night. Since then I have the keys to her apartment. I live with her when she is in Paris, which isn't often. Her job involves a lot of travel. But we manage to spend time together on idyllic tropical islands when she feels like some time off."

"Does she mind...sharing you?"

Hubert burst out laughing.

"She thinks it adds a bit of spice to our relationship. I imagine she has plenty opportunities on her side, but we never talk about it. In a sense we are both bound by professional secrecy. I've already told you too much. You are terrible, with your seemingly innocent questions!"

"It's an occupational hazard I'm afraid. What time does your Rolex say?"

"Two a.m."

"Hubert, I haven't been bored for a second, but I'd better get some sleep. Tomorrow is going to be an important day for my future career."

"As you wish, but before I leave, may I ask YOU a question?"

"Go ahead."

"I watched you with your friends during the evening, and it looked like the party didn't really matter to you. You seemed miles away. Am I wrong ?"

"You are a perceptive and sensitive observer. You'd make a good journalist."

"So I am not mistaken?"

"No. Part of me was elsewhere, you're right."

Hubert stood up and went towards her bookshelves which were laden with haphazard piles of books and picked up a photograph propped against a dictionary. He pointed to the thin-faced man with his hand on Mathilde's shoulder.

"Were you with him?"

She stiffened.

"So my friends have told you my life story!"

"Certainly not. Your expression alone gave you away. You kept looking at this photo."

"You are worse than a journalist - you have the mindset of a cop!"

He studied the photo. Mathilde sensed he looked briefly taken aback, but quickly recovered himself.

"Do you know him?"

He put the photo back on the shelf.

"No. I was just wondering what didn't look quite right about the two of you."

"Do you have any idea?"

"Perhaps. I'm sure you instinctively know the answer but won't admit it. Be brave and acknowledge it."

Mathilde lost her temper.

"Look here - you have stepped over the line. I don't need a shrink. Now, please leave."

"Just give me a moment to wash these glasses and put the bottle in the fridge..."

She stopped him: "Go away NOW!"

Hubert put his business card on the table.

"If in the future you or any of your friends need my services, do not hesitate to call. I offer good rates to regulars."

He bowed and left the apartment, closing the door noiselessly behind him.

Collapsing onto the sofa, Mathilde howled her misery into a cushion. Then she picked up the barely opened bottle and gulped it down.

CHAPTER 3

A Glimpse of Provence

The next morning, Mathilde was jolted out of a deep sleep by the sound of her telephone. Curled up on the sofa she slowly came to. Her head felt like it was in a vice, her neck was stiff and her limbs ached. She raised herself painfully. Blinding light streamed through the lounge window. She opened her eyes and promptly shut them again, groaning. The phone continued to ring, drilling into her head. Finally sitting up, she saw glasses on the coffee table and looked around for the bottle - it lay empty on the floor at her feet. All at once the evening came back to her and she winced. What time could it be? A wave of panic surged through her. When the phone stopped, the resulting silence was just as unbearable.

In the bathroom she made herself take a cold shower which succeeded in waking her properly. Naked and freezing, she studied herself uncompromisingly in the mirror - her face looked drawn, her complexion dull and her hair lacklustre. Dressing quickly and dabbing on some make-up she grabbed her bag and keys and hurried out of the apartment.

The *Rue des Martyrs* sparkled in the summer sun. Local residents strolled by with their shopping trolleys, lingering at the stalls to inspect the fruit or chat with the sellers. Mathilde ran down the street, dodging prams. It was almost ten o'clock by the time she reached the underground.

On arriving at the office she found the newsroom almost deserted. Benoît was there, tidying his desk and waiting for her.

"At last! Everyone is upstairs. Let's go - we've just got time."

They hurried upstairs. In the conference room their colleagues stood around in small groups waiting for the editor-in-chief to arrive.

"We're in luck, he's not there yet!" said Mathilde.

"I was getting worried. I left messages on your mobile and kept calling your landline."

Benoît was still a little breathless. She smelt his breath and scolded him in a low voice.

"You are not just reckless, it's suicide. Please promise me you'll see a cardiologist."

"I don't have the time."

A silence fell and the meeting commenced. The well-oiled daily ritual to decide on the day's news content never took very long. Everyone presented their topics, then the editor-in-chief announced any changes to the editorial. Benoît was applauded, the new Head of Department congratulated, then everyone promptly returned to their phone or computer.

"Benoît, I haven't thanked you for the flowers," said Mathilde, "You are a dear, you shouldn't have!"

"Are you free for lunch?"

"Yes, but I don't have long. I have a press conference early afternoon."

"In that case we can go to the Chinese restaurant across the street."

At one o'clock they managed to get a table in the crowded little restaurant.

"So you want to know how my birthday party went, is that it?" asked Mathilde with a smile once they had ordered.

Benoît flushed as he often did when his motives were exposed. Mathilde was touched but as she still held it against him for choosing Odile as his assistant, she was tempted to string him along with a different ending to her evening. They both enjoyed a flirtatious friendship which had never gone further than gestures of affection - which pleased Mathilde but did not fully satisfy Benoît. "I'm all yours, darling, just say where and when" he would say, and she would smilingly brush it aside, pretending not to take him seriously.

Over her bowl of soup she gave him an amusing account of the evening, and even suggested running a story about male escorts, although he did not appear very enthusiastic. Irritated, she left him with his coffee and rushed off to her meeting. She realised that by bringing up the subject she was actually looking for an excuse to call Hubert. His reaction to the photo had bothered her. Even though he had denied it, she was sure he knew Christophe.

Back home at the end of the day, Mathilde looked through her mail. A handwritten envelope caught her eye. It contained a short, typed letter with a scrawling signature. A lawyer from Aix-en-Provence, a certain Olivier d'Estrello, formally asked her to get in touch as soon as possible.

It was too late to call. Perhaps her mother, who had retired to Nice on becoming a widow, could satisfy her curiosity, but on the phone the day before she had not mentioned any family business requiring a lawyer.

Mathilde spent a restless night. She woke at dawn, with the unpleasant memory of the recurrent nightmare she had experienced since Christophe had left her - desperately combing the streets of an unknown town, invariably culminating in a silent face to face with Christophe, ending with him pushing her away in disgust.

She took a long, purifying shower.

At nine o'clock on the dot she called the lawyer's office on her way to work. She was told that Mr d'Estrello was on the phone and was asked if she would prefer to wait or to leave a message. She left her number. Five minutes later her mobile buzzed just as a metro arrived. She had the sudden intuition that this call was going to change her life. Instead of pushing her way into the crowded carriage, she stepped back and sat down on a platform bench.

"Olivier d'Estrello speaking."

"It's Mathilde Germain."

"I am pleased to hear from you at last, Miss Germain."

The lawyer's voice was friendly, with an amusing Southern French accent.

"What is it about?"

"I have a legal dossier that concerns you, but unfortunately I cannot divulge any details about it outside my office. You will have to come to Aix-en-Provence."

"Can you not at least give me a clue what it's about?"

"It's a bit complicated, I'm afraid. But I can assure you it is not bad news".

"Please be aware, sir, that I work for a major newspaper and it is hard for me to take a day off at a moment's notice in the middle of the week without good reason."

"I fully understand how busy you must be, like everyone else, but there is no other solution. Aix is only three hours from Paris by high speed train. It's practically a suburb - you could almost do the return trip in the day but it would be more sensible to book a room in a hotel. This particular case needs a bit of time. I'll let you think about it. Call my secretary today to fix a date. I remain at your disposal. I hope I hear from you very soon, Miss Germain."

Beside the office coffee machine she told Benoît about the intriguing phone call.

"You maybe have a forgotten aunt who has died and left you her entire estate. Imagine inheriting acres of vineyard near Aix, and a magnificent country house with a tree-lined drive," he said wistfully.

Mathilde smiled: "In your dreams, my dear friend. I have no family down there. No, I don't think it's an inheritance somehow."

"You have no choice - you'll have to go down there. Shall I come with you? I've got good friends in Marseilles."

She dodged the question.

"It's given me the idea for an article – something along the lines of *What are Lawyers actually for?* Does anybody know - do YOU?!"

"Yes, they ratify divorces," he replied sombrely, "So, leave on Friday and don't come back till Monday if you want. I'll cover for you on the Sunday. We've just completed that big assignment - you deserve a break."

She blew him a kiss.

"You are adorable, but don't take advantage of the situation and flirt with Odile!"

"No chance of that. She's in love."

"In love, *her*!

"Yes, and with a charming man – I've met him."

"So you see each other outside the office?!"

"From time to time."

"I'll never understand why you take an interest in that woman."

Benoît smiled.

"One reason is that it makes you jealous. Which might mean you fancy me just a little."

Their discussion was interrupted by Mathilde's mobile. The lawyer himself was returning her call. His warm voice sent a tremor through her and her heart pounded inexplicably.

"I'm sorry to bother you again," he said, and she noted the faint irony. "I've just remembered that it's the start of the Aix opera festival. All the hotels will be full. But I have friends who run a guest house not far from our office. They are prepared to offer you a room free of charge."

Mathilde was taken aback.

"You are really too kind. Is my dossier really that important?"

He burst out laughing.

"Your perseverance is a tribute to your professional skills, Miss Germain. But I can tell you no more over the phone. Just let me know when you are free and I will fit in."

"I could make it this coming Friday and Saturday."

"Fine. Get back to me as soon as you know when you arrive. Someone will pick you up at the station."

"I wonder what this lawyer is like," mused Mathilde after ending the call. "It's odd, but he doesn't have the voice I would expect of one."

"I've checked online," replied Benoît, "It's a big legal practice, apparently a family business. Three partners with the same name work there."

"The one who called me sounded rather young."

"You're looking all dreamy, Mattie!"

She showered him with paper clips: "Please do NOT start imagining me in the arms of a lawyer. It's hardly glamorous!"

"Who knows?"

"Anyway, he's probably married."

"I'd love to know what Olivier d'Estrello actually looks like," grinned Benoît.

"Probably balding, with a shaggy beard, dirty fingernails and a waistcoat."

Their laughter was met with glares from their colleagues conducting telephone interviews. Mathilde merely fluttered her eyelashes at them.

"That said, I'd rather picture you in the arms of a journalist," whispered Benoît.

"He'd have to be famous though."

"So I'm clearly out of the running," he sighed.

"Unless you switch to the Foreign Section!"

CHAPTER 4

Cézanne's Mont Sainte-Victoire

The high speed train sped south. Under the blinding glare of a Mediterranean sun, Mathilde contemplated a landscape dotted with wooded hills, scrubland, orchards surrounded by trim cypress hedges and villages perched on rocky summits. As they approached Aix, the landscape became gentler, with pine forests punctuated by olive groves and vineyard covered hills.

She leant her forehead against the window of the airconditioned carriage, instinctively seeking freshness. Since leaving Paris that morning she had been prey to conflicting emotions. Unable to concentrate on her book, she kept wondering what was awaiting her in this strange town. She sensed it would be life changing.

Alighting at the Aix high-speed train station lost in the middle of the countryside, she wished she had swapped her jeans for a summer dress. At ten o'clock in the morning the heat was already stifling. She looked around for her welcome committee. The lawyer had not given clear details. People bustled round her. Clinging to her travel bag, she felt like a lost little girl. Strangely, she was close to tears. Her reaction was all the more surprising given that she spent her life travelling and was no stranger to the unexpected. She put her weakness down to fatigue and settled down to wait.

The arrivals hall had almost completely emptied when a vivacious brunette bounced up to her smiling broadly.

"You must be Miss Germain!"

Mathilde nodded.

"Véronique Bianchi" she announced, stretching out her hand, "I am Mr d'Estrello's assistant. I hope you haven't been waiting too long. There was a road accident."

"It's really very kind of Mr d'Estrello to send me a driver," replied Mathilde, already won over.

"I presume you know Aix."

"No, this is my first time here."

"In that case you should start by admiring our famous emblem," declared Véronique pointing to an asymmetrically shaped mountain on the horizon, its slopes white in the glare of the heat.

Another wave of emotion overwhelmed Mathilde. Seen at an angle, the mountain ridge rose protectively, its steepest slope jutting onto a wooded plateau. She was familiar with Mont Sainte-Victoire, so often painted by Cézanne, but never imagined that this iconic mass of rocks would have such an effect on her. It was as if this mountain had always dwelt somewhere inside her and that now, years later, she had found a long lost friend from whom she had only just parted.

"It's in the evening that the light is at its kindest," continued Véronique, aware of Mathilde's emotion.

"It's magnificent, much lovelier in reality than Cézanne's depictions of it."

Véronique burst out laughing.

"Olivier would love to hear that. He just adores Mont Sainte-Victoire, but I warn you he's also a great fan of Cézanne. Come this way, my car is just over there, the black convertible. Get in. I'll fold back the roof if you don't mind."

"Not at all.'

"What was the weather like in Paris?"

"Overcast!"

"I could never live in the north of France. Down here we would fade away if we didn't have our daily dose of sunshine."

"It's what you're used to," said Mathilde more crisply than she intended, "I was born in Paris, I've always lived there and have never thought of living anywhere else."

"Just as well. Imagine if all the Northerners moved down here! Oh dear, I'd better watch what I say, Olivier wouldn't like it. You must find me on over familiar terms with my employer, but I've known him since he was a kid, plus that's what our office is like. I should explain the situation: there are three d'Estrello lawyers in the practice - the father and his two sons Olivier and Frédéric. To avoid confusion we tend to use first names. I usually work for Olivier, the elder son. Between you and me he's the nicest! Mind you, I shouldn't be telling you all this - I really do talk too much."

Dazzled by the bright light, Mathilde, who, on her hasty departure that morning had left her sunglasses behind, closed her eyes. In her mind's eye she saw Christophe floating against the kaleidoscopic patterns made by the sunlight. Her heart sank and she only heard bits of what her driver was recounting.

They reached the outskirts of Aix.

"You'll be staying in the Mazarin district, the nicest part of the city in my opinion," announced Véronique.

"Take the time to walk around. You'll see some lovely town houses and baroque fountains. Feel free to open those big doors - there are beautiful gardens hidden inside. You won't regret it."

She double-parked the convertible in a narrow street in front of a tall ochre-coloured building, its stonework crumbling in places.

"Here we are. I can't stay long, I'm blocking the road. Your appointment is at half past eleven. Do you see that boulevard at the end of the street? Our office is on the corner, you can't miss it. See you in a little while."

.

Véronique set off at speed, waving goodbye. Mathilde used the heavy bronze door knocker. An elegantly dressed man opened the huge door and showed her in. The flagstone hall was blissfully cool and led to a majestic terracotta staircase with a wrought iron banister. He picked up her travel bag and asked him to follow her.

"Your room is under the eaves, but do not worry, there is air-conditioning."

He led the way to the third floor. On the way up she paused to admire the contemporary art on the walls.

"If you require anything at all please let me know," said her host showing her into her room.

Mathilde nodded with a smile. The room was small but tastefully decorated. It opened onto a large terrace decked with chaise longues and which looked out over the tiled rooves of the old town. The air was sweet with the scent of laurel and white geraniums growing in the large glazed terracotta tubs. She stretched like a cat in the sun. How lovely it would be to spend the evening in this enchanting place, reading and watching the town turn pink in the setting sun. Reluctantly she went back inside. She had just enough time for a quick shower before her appointment. She quickly changed. In the afternoon she would go out and buy a dress, sandals and sunglasses. At the bathroom mirror she tied back her long blond hair and touched up her makeup. She thought she was looking better.

Outside on the sunny pavement she felt as if she was at last emerging from a long dark tunnel. She crossed a shady square lined with plane trees and beautiful old houses, in the middle of which stood a round fountain with four stone dolphins with raised fins. In the car Véronique had mentioned that the dolphins had 'scales like fish'. Mathilde came closer and surreptitiously stroked one. An old man who was sitting on the edge of the basin gave her a gap-toothed grin.

"Go ahead, Mademoiselle – it'll bring you luck!"

If he knew how much I need it!

"You're not from around here, I can tell. Throw some coins into the fountain and one day you'll return to our beautiful city and find happiness."

He uttered his pronouncement slowly and distinctly. Mathilde did as he asked.

"Now give me a smile and everything will turn out right, you'll see, my lovely."

She gave him a dazzling smile.

"You've made my day. See you keep that Madonna smile on your pretty face. The best of luck!" He waved goodbye as she tripped off with a light step.

The legal practice was located in an imposing grey stone building. At the reception desk in the lobby she was ceremoniously ushered into the waiting room at the back of the building where several clients sat reading newspapers or studying documents. The ground floor windows gave onto tree-filled grounds and a car park. Among the smart cars she spotted a red Porsche glinting in the sun. She had no time to wonder who might own it, because Véronique's friendly face appeared at the door.

"Mr d'Estrello, is ready to receive you. Please follow me."

She jumped up, her heart pounding.

Ignoring a series of padded doors, Véronique headed for the stairs. As if reading Mathilde's mind she whispered:

"Olivier doesn't handle prestigious dossiers, so he's relegated to the second floor. Mind you, I think he prefers it. So do I!"

The dream of a country house with vineyards, innocently planted in her mind by Benoît promptly evaporated. She tried to keep the smile on her face. Véronique knocked on the half open office door.

She heard a friendly "Come in!"

After a moment's hesitation she stepped inside and the door closed behind her.

The room was plunged in darkness. A tall figure approached with a hand outstretched. Mathilde, who was herself almost six feet tall (too tall, she felt), calculated that he must be at least six inches taller than her. She was taken aback.

"Welcome, Mademoiselle Germain. I'm sorry if I startled you. The room has no air-conditioning and in summer I have to close the shutters. We could find a cooler room for our meeting if you want."

"Please don't bother. I hate air-conditioning and don't mind it here. But I'm a bit claustrophobic. If you could open the shutters a little it would be better."

"Of course!"

As the lawyer did so, he gave a muffled cry of pain and Mathilde imagined he had pinched his fingers. She stifled a laugh at his clumsiness.

With some light now entering the room she saw a tall man in a badly fitting crumpled linen suit. When she ventured to glance at his face her hopes were dashed - Olivier d'Estrello in person did not live up to his seductive voice. He had a thatch of shaggy brown hair and his features were not particularly attractive. He looked at her sombrely behind old-fashioned horn-rimmed glasses.

"Did you have a good trip?"

"Excellent, thank you."

At least he has a nice smile, or is he being ironic?

Unaware of his visitor's scrutiny he opened a file.

Intelligent hands. No wedding ring!

"Now you will finally find out why you have come here! You have received a donation. I must read out the whole document verbatim. I assure you it won't take too long. Would you like a coffee or a cold drink?"

"A glass of water would be fine."

He called for Véronique, adjusted his glasses, cleared his throat and started to read. Lulled by his melodious accent, Mathilde learned to her astonishment that a certain David Stevenson, Professor of History of Art, born on 14th March 1952 in Boston, Massachusetts and living in Washington DC, had gifted to Mademoiselle Mathilde Marie Germain, Journalist, born on 4th July 1985 in Paris, a property located in Saint-Marc-Jaumegarde, Bouches-du-Rhône, comprising four hectares of land including a house measuring one hundred square metres.

The standard legalese was delivered in the same impersonal tone: "*...Duly signed this Day, 15th June 2015 at the office of Olivier d'Estrello, Lawyer, Aix-en-Provence.*"

He took a leisurely sip of water and looked straight at Mathilde:

"Do you have any questions?"

"Lots!"

"Go ahead, what is the first one?"

"Who is this Stevenson? - I've never heard of him!"

"An American university professor."

"Thank you, I'm not deaf."

A faint smile escaped the lawyer.

He's got sensual lips. I wonder what his kisses taste like?

"Why is he not here today?"

"He is not required to attend. The document has already been signed here."

She raised a hand to interrupt him: "But why donate this to ME?"

"Mr Stevenson did not disclose his motives. From the legal perspective, anyone may dispose of their property as they see fit."

"He must have picked the wrong person!"

The lawyer picked up the ID she had submitted on arriving.

"Are you Mathilde Marie Germain, born on..."

"Yes" she interrupted sharply.

His smile broadened and his eyes twinkled.

"In that case there is absolutely no doubt about it."

If only he wasn't wearing these awful spectacles! How can he have such poor taste?!

Mr d'Estrello removed his glasses, polished them slowly with a large handkerchief and before putting them back on he gazed at Mathilde who flushed.

"Mr Stevenson simply asked me to show you round the property he is gifting to you and indicated that after the visit you will have some answers to your questions."

"Is that what lawyers are for?"

"How do you mean?"

"To carry out instructions from crazy clients?!"

"Mr Stevenson seemed to me to be of sound mind. If you want we can go to the property at once," continued Olivier unperturbed, "unless you would like to eat something first."

"I'm not hungry."

"In that case I suggest we have a picnic after seeing round the place. It's in an idyllic spot, you'll see."

His eyes behind his spectacles twinkled and suddenly Mathilde found him charming. He took a bunch of keys from an envelope.

"Let's go then."

She followed him to his car. An old Volvo, its roof folded back, was parked next to the Porsche.

"That magnificent red car belongs to my brother," he said, answering the question she had been longing to ask.

He gallantly opened the passenger door for her then went to the driver's seat. Inside there was a smell of old wood and damp dog.

"My car is not exactly spotless, I do apologise. I live in the country and use it to transport all sorts of things."

"Where are we going?"

"To Saint-Marc-Jaumegarde, near Mont Sainte-Victoire. It's not very far."

Mathilde felt a tremor of shock run through her and bit her lips. So she was right - that mysterious mountain played a mysterious role in her life, and she was about to know why. She longed to call Benoît and tell him everything.

On the way the lawyer stopped at a roadside stall and returned with a large brown paper bag.

"Our lunch!" he announced, "100% organic."

"So you're a 'greenie!" teased his passenger.

"I'm first a farmer and, to be specific, an olive grower, so naturally I respect the environment."

She turned to him in astonishment.

"But I thought you were a lawyer!"

"Only in my spare time. I studied law and became a lawyer mainly because it's a family tradition, but also because it makes good money and doesn't take up too much time. My father obligingly hands me the simplest cases."

"Like mine!"

He laughed loudly: "I have a feeling, Miss Germain, that your dossier may well be the trickiest of my whole career."

He started up the engine, the gearbox grinding noisily.

Heading east, the road quickly became narrow and winding. At each bend Mont Sainte-Victoire appeared and disappeared as if by magic.

Her lawyer seemed very happy, humming as he drove along. After a few miles the Volvo turned up a track which ended in a cul-de-sac, and pulled up in the shade of a tree.

"We'll have to walk a bit. Do you have proper shoes?"

She showed him her flat pumps but he made no comment.

He had a good look at my legs!

He filled a battered backpack from the car boot with their picnic.

"OK, let's go," he said on replacing his scruffy suede moccasins with a pair of well used hiking boots. He donned a cap and handed her one.

"Wear it - you'll need it."

Mathilde waved it away.

"It's easy to see you are not from around here, *Mademoiselle*," he teased, "The sun is fierce at this time of day. If you don't cover your head you'll flake out."

He made another attempt to give it to her.

"No thanks!"

"As you wish."

They set off along a wooded path which got narrower and narrower, with broken branches and overturned stumps making it impassable at times. Olivier quite naturally took hold of Mathilde's hand to help her past the difficult bits.

They eventually emerged into a clearing at the end of which was the house, bathed in sunlight. Mathilde gasped. Behind it, the mysterious mountain could be seen face on - a long limestone ridge punctuated by outcrops and ravines. She stood transfixed. A few seconds later, she realised that he was still holding her hand. At that moment he let go. A white cloud passed over the mountain, instantly making it look darker. Mathilde shivered. Her fingers inadvertently brushed Olivier's leg. He turned to her and saw her smiling beatifically.

"Thank you for showing me this magical place," she blurted.

"It's David Stevenson you should be thanking. But I'm pleased you are receptive to the charm of the place."

Their eyes met. Olivier smiled disarmingly.

He pointed to the high rounded summit.

"That's the *Pic des Mouches,* it's over a thousand metres high. From the top you can see across to the snowy foothills of the Alps on the one side and the Mediterranean on the other. I know it well - one day I'd like to take you there."

He's looking ahead, as if we will quite naturally continue to see each other. Can he be falling in love with me?!

Side by side, without touching, they approached the house - a low south-facing building with crudely grouted stone walls.

"The house is not damp but don't expect great comfort. It is not connected to the grid. It's more of a holiday home - a *campagne* they called it in Cézanne's time."

"Did he come here to paint?"

"Probably, but he preferred to paint the mountain from the side, at its most cubist angle."

Olivier unlocked the door and pushed it open.

"Are you ready, Miss Germain?"

"Ready for what?"

"To solve the mystery."

"I think so."

He stepped aside to let Mathilde enter.

"David Stevenson wanted you to discover the house on your own."

She stepped back nervously.

"There might be scorpions or snakes inside."

"I doubt it. But would you like me to check?"

"Yes please," she piped in a childish voice.

She waited at the threshold. A few seconds later, Olivier emerged triumphantly.

"Apart from a few harmless spiders, the path is now clear."

Strands of cobweb were stuck to his hair.

"They lured you into their web" she laughed.

He shook himself like a dog. Timidly she brushed off the remaining streaks.

"My fingers are all sticky now," she smiled.

Olivier held her wrist and carefully wiped her fingertips with his handkerchief.

He has soft hands. He's nice and gentle. Do I attract him?

"It's not the time to back out now."

"I'm scared stiff."

"I understand. It's just the first step that's hard."

Mathilde trembled.

"I'll wait for you under the fig tree," said Olivier and loped off with long supple strides, "I forgot to tell you, the house is called *Le Mas du Figuier*."

CHAPTER 5

Le Mas du Figuier

The house was filled with a gentle light. Olivier had already opened the shutters. Mathilde found herself in the main room dominated by a stone fireplace which still contained a pile of partly burnt logs. The air smelt of cold ash and Provence herbs. Sprigs of dried thyme, lavender and rosemary hung from the beams, threatening to turn into dust if touched. The place felt neglected but exuded a reassuring peacefulness. Mathilde, in tune with the spirit of houses, felt that its occupants had been happy here. A shaft of light poured through the heart-shaped aperture in the shutters and landed on the dark flagstones.

The room contained a long old pine table, with wicker chairs round it. A few mismatched plates, some chipped bowls and two brass spoons still lay on an ancient wooden dish rack on the wall.

Mathilde bent her head to enter the next room through the low door, thinking that Olivier must have had to bend almost double to get through. A large bed covered with a faded quilted bedspread took up almost the whole room. Books lined the walls. Mathilde picked one up at random - it was *Travels with a Donkey* by Robert Louis Stevenson. It struck her as weird that the author's name was the same as that of the owner of the house, and the fact that it was one of her own favourite books.

In a dark corner of the bedroom a metal three-legged dressing table with an oval mirror caught her eye. A photo was propped against the mirror. Mathilde picked it up without even glancing at it and slipped it into the pocket of her jeans. There was no point exploring any further, she felt.

On the doorstep the midday heat struck her with full force. Dazzled by the light, she shaded her eyes and searched for Olivier. She found him stretched out under the old fig tree, apparently dozing. She ran to join him, the earth molten hot beneath her feet. In the shade of the tree it was almost as hot. She collapsed on the rug beside him.

"I'm so thirsty!"

He raised himself on one elbow and offered her a battered flask. She gulped down the metallic but deliciously cold water.

"Thank you!"

She lay down and gazed dreamily at the dappled light through the broad leaves of the fig tree.

"Are you hungry now?" inquired Olivier solicitously.

"Not really."

"You have to eat, you are as pale as a Madonna. I'm sure you haven't eaten a thing since this morning."

"I got up really early to catch the train."

"I'm dying of hunger myself."

He produced a crusty loaf, two misshapen tomatoes, some small goat cheeses and peaches from his bag and spread it all out in front of them. Then he brought out a well-worn penknife.

"I wouldn't mind a tomato," conceded Mathilde.

He cut one in two and sprinkled it with olive oil from an unmarked bottle.

She sunk her teeth into it, the juice dribbling down her chin and neck.

"It's delicious, it's like biting into the sun! And that oil is heavenly. You make it yourself, don't you?"

He nodded, gently dabbing the juice still trickling down her face with his handkerchief. She could see his contentment reflected in his eyes.

It's so easy to make a man happy. Why was I not able to manage with Christophe? What didn't I do? Where did I go wrong?

"Do you ever come to Paris on business?"

"I hardly ever leave my home."

"That's a pity. If ever you have the chance, I could show you my favourite haunts - hidden gardens and unspoilt natural havens," Mathilde heard herself saying.

Here I am imagining a future with this man who I didn't even know a mere two hours ago! What's happening to me?

"Do you know that vines grow not far from where I live, on the slopes of Montmartre?"

Propped on one elbow he watched her as she toyed with a blade of grass.

"I'll come one day, that's a promise."

Mathilde removed her pumps and twiddled her varnished toenails.

"You have spiritual feet," he ventured.

"You know how to talk to a woman! People usually tell me my feet are too big! I'll remember your description!" she laughingly retorted.

She suddenly felt sleepy and stifled a yawn.

"You're right, the sun is strong. I'd love a little nap."

She lay back, her arms crossed behind her head and enjoyed a moment of peace she hadn't experienced for months. *Was it the protective aura of the mountainside or the presence of this calm strong man?* She began to understand his attachment to the region, his roots and his accent.

She half hoped, half feared he would stretch out beside her. However, he did no such thing, he merely gathered up the remains of their meal and packed up. When her phone buzzed deep inside her bag she did not rush to answer it. Benoît's name showed on the screen. She rejected the call and turned her phone off. Only a few hours ago she couldn't live without her phone.

What's happening to me? she wondered again.

Christophe's ghost was gradually fading, she was at last moving on.

"Would you fancy trying that?" asked Olivier, pointing to a paraglider.

"No way! I have vertigo."

"And if I was with you? Some can take two people you know."

"You don't know what you're asking of me!"

"Sorry! I tend to be over enthusiastic when it comes to my passions. But I don't give up easily. I'm sure that one day I'll have the pleasure of showing you my region from the air."

Mathilde felt bewildered. Since falling for Olivier's dulcet tones on the phone, everything was starting to move too fast. Above them the paraglider wound slowly downwards on the air currents. She sat up abruptly, in a confusion of emotions.

"I don't want to take up too much of your time. You surely have a busy schedule."

"No, I've kept this afternoon aside for you."

And now I've gone and disappointed him!

Olivier put on his backpack and helped Mathilde up. Suddenly she remembered the photo in her pocket. She showed it to him.

"I found this in the bedroom. I haven't even looked at it properly, I'd almost forgotten about it. It might be the answer to the mystery."

"Would you like me to let you study it in peace?"

"I don't know" she said.

Again she felt bewildered.

"I'll go and close the shutters and lock up. I won't be long."

Her hand trembling, Mathilde raised the photo to her eyes. She saw a young couple, the woman she immediately recognised was her mother, nestling against a blond male stranger who gazed at her as she laughed into the camera. She was stunned. The man looked so like herself, she couldn't deny it although her whole being rejected the fact. Trying to recover her composure she took a look at the back of the photo. It bore the words *Le Mas du Figuier, 11th Oct.*

1984, Micheline & David. She immediately worked out that the photo was presumably taken by a friend of the couple about nine months before she was born!

Olivier returned just in time to catch her in his arms as she fainted. Tenderly he carried his light but precious burden to the car, thinking all the way that he could have gladly carried her to the end of the world. This David Stevenson may have been a seducer, but he had made Olivier d'Estrello the happiest of men.

He placed Mathilde on the back seat of the Volvo, fanned her and bathed her face with the rest of the water in his flask. As she failed to regain consciousness, he gently slapped her cheeks. She opened her eyes, startled to see this person leaning anxiously and unflatteringly over her. Olivier sensed that she was trying to remember who he was.

"What happened?" she groaned.

"Sunstroke I think."

Mathilde realised she was still gripping the photograph.

"Don't make fun of me!"

He was pleased she had regained her verve even if he was on the receiving end.

"I am not making fun of you. I am simply pleased that your face has regained some colour."

She glared at him.

"Now, tell me the truth, Mr d'Estrello – is the man in this photo the same person who came to your office?"

She brandished it but would not let him hold it. With one hand he held her wrist and with the other he lifted his spectacles to examine the photograph.

"What weird problems do you have with your eyesight?" she giggled, "Do you know that those glasses don't suit you at all?"

"Yes, that's him, give or take a few wrinkles. Actually, he hasn't changed that much."

"Do you think, as I do, that David Stevenson is my father?"

"I'm astigmatic. I don't see clearly either close up or distance."

"Since you're not answering my question, I'm going to call my mother this instant."

She rummaged in her bag for her phone.

"Math... Miss Germain, I'm not sure you're in the right mood for a sensible conversation with your mother at the moment."

"Are you implying that I'm not sensible?!"

"Merely exhausted."

"You're an unconvincing liar. You'd have made a poor barrister."

"I never intended to be one."

He looks upset. I've spoiled everything, as usual!

Olivier fastened her seatbelt and went round to the driver's seat.

"I'll take you back to the guest house so you can have a rest in your room and calm down a bit before deciding what to do."

He turned on the radio.

"You must hate me and you're right," she said after a while, "I'm really horrid to you, and I don't know why. I can't help it. I presume I'm making you pay for all the men who have let me down. And because you seem able to take it I've let myself go. The day I apologise, it'll be for real."

"I'm not holding it against you. You're upset."

"I can't tell you how much!"

"I'd like to be able to help."

"You are a nice man."

"Coming from a woman, it's rarely a compliment."

"When I say it, it is. Keep being nice to me, Mr d'Estrello, I really need it."

They arrived at the hotel. Olivier parked illegally in the *Place des Quatre Dauphins* and helped Mathilde out of the car.

"Back to square one," she said.

"Are you OK? Would you like me to accompany you to the door?"

"I'd appreciate that."

She clung to him. At the hotel entrance, he appeared to hesitate.

"I'll see you in my office tomorrow morning. You have an important decision to make and there are a few formalities to complete."

He made as if to leave then turned back.

"I have two seats for the opera this evening at the Archevêché – a performance of *Don Giovanni.* I was wondering if..."

"It would be with great pleasure."

His eyes lit up with surprise and delight, like a little boy with an unexpected treat. Mathilde was touched. *How many women had lamely turned down his invitations simply because he was too 'nice' or not glamorous enough?*

A traffic warden was approaching their car.

"I think you'd better hurry," she said.

"See you this evening. Don't hesitate to call if you need anything."

He strode back to the Volvo. From the entrance she watched him negotiate with the traffic warden, then discreetly turn to give her the victory sign.

CHAPTER 6

End of Act One

Back in her room, Mathilde went onto her terrace and stretched out on a chaise longue under the parasol. She turned on her phone, her heart thumping. Her mother answered with her customary casualness. Mathilde appreciated how she didn't intrude in her private life but this time she felt betrayed. She deserved to know the truth and had braced herself to hear it. Leaving the legal details aside, she described the visit to the farmhouse and her revelation. A silence followed.

"Mother, are you still there?"

"Of course, came the reply, choked with emotion.

"Do you confirm that David Stevenson is my biological father?"

"I'd rather you came to Nice to hear about it all. It's a long story, dear Mathilde."

"It's too late," Mathilde retorted sharply, "I need to know the truth now, and to be honest I'd rather hear it from a distance."

"If that's what you want. There is no doubt that David is your father. You were conceived in the farmhouse you've just visited."

It was Mathilde's turn to fall silent.

"Are you still there, darling?"

"But I had a father. I loved him. Did he ever realise I was not his daughter?"

"I never hid it from him. When I told him he took it with his customary tact. And he loved you like his own daughter – you were the best present I had ever given him, he often said to me. After you I had several miscarriages, as you know."

Mathilde's throat tightened - her mother had never opened up about her grief at losing an unborn child.

"And David?"

"By the time I found out I was pregnant he had already left for the States. I didn't think it was a good idea to tell him."

"Did you love him?"

"I was in love with him, I think there's a subtle difference. The person I really loved and who I cherished right until the end was the man who called you his daughter."

Mathilde could understand that one could love two men at the same time but had trouble accepting that her mother would have cheated like that.

She ploughed on with her questions.

"How does David know I exist?"

"A few weeks after your father died I called him."

"Without telling me first?!"

"I'd no idea how he would react. I knew he was married with kids and still lived in the States. Plus, if he refused to believe me it was better if you knew nothing about it."

Mathilde held her breath.

"And then?"

Her mother hesitated.

"It was a brief conversation. I imagine his wife was close by. He didn't sound very pleased to hear me and I didn't insist. Then a few days later he called me back simply to ask me what name we had given you. He also wanted me to send some photos. That was the last time I spoke to him. I thought he would leave it at that. That's why I didn't tell you about it. There was no way I imagined he would decide to give you the farmhouse. I actually thought he'd sold it a long time ago."

"It all feels such a waste," blurted Mathilde. "Why didn't you just keep the secret to yourself?"

"Please calm down, darling. After your father's death you seemed so alone, so lost. I thought perhaps..."

"Do you realise how distraught I feel now though?" interrupted Mathilde, "not to mention how shocked David must have been - and his family."

"My dear, we are rarely aware of the effect of our actions. We are driven by motives that are more powerful than any logic. It's human nature. It's too late to turn the clock back now. I just hope that David's initiative will lead to something else, and that you will have a chance to meet him and his other children. That is my dearest wish. David is a precious part of my past, I accept that and want it to keep the memory intact. I have only one piece of advice for you, dear Mathilde, which is to love, and love without counting the cost. It will always bring you some happiness."

Mathilde hung up, somewhat reassured. Try as she might, she couldn't blame her mother whose poise and determination reflected admirable resilience. She knew this was a real strength, which would serve her well in life.

Later, Mathilde went out to buy a dress. She wanted to feel desirable - which hadn't happened for a very long time. For months now, she had put up with Christophe's unresponsive face, refusing to accept that he no longer loved her.

Now she wanted to ignite the flame of desire in a man, and Olivier's eyes had burned promisingly.

In a chic boutique she fell for a ridiculously expensive silk mousseline dress which made her look very sexy. The sales assistant had no trouble convincing her to swap her pumps for outrageously high stilettos. They looked hard to walk in but she'd been dreaming of shoes like that for so long! Christophe was slightly shorter than her and would only let her wear flat heels. A man as tall as Olivier allowed her to indulge her fantasies.

That evening, watching her perched on her high heels Olivier tried to disguise a smile.

"How do I look?" she asked, twirling in front of him.

"Sublime. But I assure you, it was not necessary to go to all that trouble for me."

She rolled her eyes. *Clearly, he doesn't understand women.*

"Charming! May I say, Mr d'Estrello, that I haven't gone to all this trouble just for you. It's also for all the other men who will cross our path this evening and who will envy you, not to mention all the women who will wonder where I found my dress, and who will go round all the shops in Aix tomorrow looking for it."

"Don't you have a shawl?" he asked, pretending he hadn't heard.

Mathilde sighed.

"You're hopeless! Hasn't your mother taught you anything?!"

"She taught me to care about the well-being of others. Here the evenings are still warm but once night falls it suddenly gets chilly."

"Well, in that case you can warm me up," she cried playfully, and smiled at his discomfiture.

As they set off, Mathilde realised that her choice of shoes was a big mistake. Several times Olivier had to stop her falling over, then decided to offer her a life-saving arm. Clutching him for support, she quickly regained a semblance of dignity. She saw passers-by turning to look at them, and had to admit that, contrary to all expectations, they must make an attractive couple, matched not only in size but in elegance too. Olivier was transformed in his dark, well cut suit. He had obviously rushed to the hairdressers. Apart from his spectacles and garish pocket handkerchief (which she hastily removed), he looked just fine.

They crossed *Cours Mirabeau,* a broad avenue thronged with bustling cafés and took a short cut through narrow streets to the archbishop's palace –

the venue each summer for opera lovers (and Mozart-lovers in particular). Along the way, Mathilde admired the picturesque squares, fountains, facades and doorways. At this time of year the town was particularly lovely, as her guide enthusiastically pointed out.

Outside the entrance to the Palace, an elegant crowd of festival goers was already gathering. Once inside the courtyard where the open-air event was staged, he led her to the upper terrace. On the way Mathilde amused herself looking at the audience and recognised a few celebrities trying hard to get noticed. She didn't particularly like opera but the idea of being in the right place at the right time appealed. Plus, she wanted to please the person accompanying her - she owed him that at least.

The austere facade of the palace served as the stage set. As the music started a silence fell, broken only by the rasping of a single cicada. Mathilde fell under the spell of the spectacle. By the time Leporello, Don Giovanni's valet, was listing his master's female conquests, she discovered she was shivering with cold. Dusk had turned into a cold starry night. Olivier tenderly wrapped the tartan rug from the seat over her. As his fingers brushed her neck a shiver of delight ran through her.

"Thank you," she whispered, "but I'm still a bit cold."

"Shh!" came a protest from behind.

Olivier put his arm round her and she nestled against him. She dropped her head, closed her eyes and concentrated on the beauty of the voices.

Thunderous applause roused her from her blissful state. Had she fallen asleep? She had an impression that at several points Olivier had stroked her forehead. She lifted her head and asked:

"Is it finished already?"

He laughed.

"If you hadn't fallen asleep you'd know it's the end of Act One.'

"I wasn't asleep,' she protested, "I was listening!"

"If you're tired I can take you back to your guest house."

"No, no. But I'm thirsty."

"The intermission lasts long enough to make it to the Members' tent."

His tallness made it easy for them to wending their way through the crowd to the VIP tent, complete with buffet and cloth-covered tables. They were hailed by a group of young people drinking champagne. As one of them approached, Mathilde noticed Olivier's face darken.

"Well, aren't you going to introduce us?" said the stranger, staring at her brazenly.

"Of course. This is my brother Frédéric d'Estrello."

"Mathilde Germain" she said crisply, holding out her hand.

"Delighted to meet you *Mademoiselle.* Would you like to join us?"

Mathilde looked inquiringly at Olivier.

"Come quickly before my friends finish off all the champagne" said Frédéric.

She followed him, with Olivier taking up the rear. The group moved aside to include them. She found herself with a glass of champagne in her hand and slipped easily into the urbane conversation around her, with its light-hearted jokes and laughter.

Frédéric d'Estrello took pride of place among the gaggle of glamorous looking women and men. He had dark hair like Olivier but was considerably smaller and edgier, contrasting with his brother's calm. His blue eyes lingered on Mathilde, indifferent to the presence of Olivier who stood a little apart, listening and not talking. At length Frédéric went up to his brother and said audibly "Where did you find such a ravishing creature? Most unusual for you I'd say!"

He received no reply. Then the bell sounded, summoning everyone back to their seats. The little group headed outside. Frédéric asked where they were seated and Mathilde gestured vaguely towards the terrace.

"Those aren't the best seats. There are some empty ones near us. Why not come and join us?"

Olivier hesitated for a moment, and his brother took the opportunity to take Mathilde's arm and get her a seat next to his by moving everyone along. When she turned to find Olivier she saw him standing immobile at the end of the now full row, looking disconcerted.

"Sit down!" shouted an irritated spectator.

The stage showed a street in Seville at night.

CHAPTER 7

Cicadas in Saint-Germain-des-Prés

Frédéric popped his head round his brother's half open office door.

"It's boiling in here! I only hope you don't make your clients sit in here. When are you going to join Father and me in more temperate climes?!"

"Never!" fumed Olivier.

"Brother dear, are you still in a bad mood from last night?"

"Get out!"

"All right. By the way, have you heard from your young protćgćc?"

Olivier stood up and lunged at his brother who remained prudently close to the exit.

"How often must I repeat myself?"

Frédéric raised his hands in a gesture of surrender but also to protect himself.

"Hey, calm down, don't get so uptight. You're like an angry wounded bull waiting for the final death blow!"

"I am indeed an angry wounded bull - go ahead, but I'll hit you back. How long has it been since our last fight?"

His brother smiled.

"At least fifteen years. You were twenty and me seventeen."

"Do you remember the reason for it?"

"Yes, as if it was yesterday. You reproached me for pinching your girlfriend when actually she made the first move. I didn't need to do a thing, and you did nothing to stop her".

"You bastard!"

"Olivier, we aren't kids any more. I've come to tell you that I'm sorry for what happened last night. It wasn't premeditated. After the performance we looked for you everywhere. You'd disappeared and your phone was turned off. I swear that I didn't lay a finger on your big-footed Mathilde. If I'd tried anything I think she would have bitten me. Actually, I think she's quite a handful - rather a difficult character."

Olivier clenched his fist: "Another word out of you and I'll sock you."

The threat didn't deter Frédéric.

"She refused to go with us to a nightclub so, like a good little boy, I drove her back to her place in my

Porsche. She sat there gritting her teeth the whole way. If anyone should be feeling guilty it's you. You've let your prey escape as usual and this time it's a real pity because for once she looked up for it…"

"You're lucky I abhor violence because otherwise I'd knock you for six! Get out of my way."

Olivier pushed past his brother and ran down the stairs. He rushed to the guest house, only to be told that Mathilde had left by taxi at dawn for the train station. No, she hadn't left a message, and she had insisted on paying the bill."

Back in the street he looked at his watch. Eleven o'clock. Mathilde would already be in Paris. Should he call her? What could he say to her? She would probably hang up on him or call him a cad and she would be right. He sat down on the edge of the Dolphins fountain where an old man was dozing in the sun.

"What an idiot I was," he groaned, "I've lost her for ever. My brother is right. I'm incapable of holding onto a woman. I'm thirty-five, I'm an unattractive bitter old bachelor. No-one will ever love me. I'll never have children to teach them all I know about Nature and Mankind."

He banged his forehead against one of the dolphins. His mutterings woke the old man.

"That'll bring you luck," he said, "but it works even better if you toss in a few coins."

Olivier rummaged in his pocket and pressed a note into the gap-toothed man's hand.

"You'd be better saving your stories for someone else, old man. I no longer believe in happiness."

Back home, Mathilde tried to sleep. The night before and all morning she had hoped against hope Olivier might call. Maybe it was just as well he didn't care about what happened to her - he was spineless and not much better than his show-off brother.

May they both go to the devil and burn in hell like Don Giovanni!

Stretched out on her sofa she tried to analyse the events of the day before, her professional training telling her to be objective. But how could she avoid this emotional turmoil!? In a single day she had found out she had an American father, had seen her mother fall from her pedestal and had imagined she was in love with a shy, not even very good-looking lawyer.

I'm being unfair, he's not that bad. He just needs a little tweaking. Anyway, what does it matter? Christophe used to criticise me for wanting to change people instead of accepting them the way they were.

Mathilde waited for the wave of pain she usually felt on being reminded of her lost love. But in her imagination she kept seeing Olivier's face. Soothed by the caring warmth he exuded she fell asleep.

On waking she saw Hubert's business card lying discarded on the table and her laughter echoed round the silent apartment.

Among the messy upheavals in my life I must remember other memorable moments. On my thirtieth birthday my best friend discarded me, a naked stranger walked around my apartment and I got drunk on my own for the first time in my life! Well done Mattie, don't you think all that is rather a lot for one person? Mathilde is rock-solid, isn't she, Christophe? You can give her lots of knocks - she might sway a little but she won't fall (unless it's into her lawyer's arms, but that was due to the effect of the sun).

She got up, took a lengthy shower, made some tea and brought it into the lounge. The card perched precariously on the edge of the table taunted her. Without thinking she grabbed her phone. Hubert answered at once, sounding unsurprised and even rather pleased.

"Am I disturbing you?"

"Not at all. How are you doing, Mathilde?"

She swallowed hard, took a deep breath and said:

"I'm alone, confused and I'd like to talk to you, but not on the phone."

"In that case when?"

"Is now possible?"

She was surprised to hear herself using the little girl voice she used as a child to win round her father.

"That's fine," he answered after a pause, "where shall we meet. At your place?"

"No, I'd prefer a café somewhere."

"Any particular one?"

"Not really."

"In that case see you at Flore's café in an hour. I'll be waiting inside."

That sunny Saturday afternoon, the terrace of Flore's on *Boulevard Saint-Germain* was crowded. Mathilde slipped discretely inside where it was blissfully quiet. There was hardly anyone there. A waiter in a long apron was leaning against the counter looking bored. She quickly spotted Hubert. He got to his feet as she came in.

"I've chosen Sartre's table," he said, "I hope you don't mind."

"He's not my favourite author, but that's fine."

The waiter came up. They ordered China tea and a somewhat banal conversation ensued.

"I'm just back from Aix-en-Provence," announced Mathilde.

"Tell me all!"

Sipping her tea she recounted her recent adventure. Hubert appeared genuinely interested, laughing loudly at her description of Olivier d'Estrello.

"He wears bifocals, gets his hair cut by his cleaning lady and his clothes look like they've come from his father's wardrobe. Oh, and I was about to forget, he's also half deaf."

"So now you are the owner of a few acres of land at the foot of an iconic mountain in Provence. I wonder if you realise how lucky you are! It's a marvellous birthday present, isn't it?"

"The land cannot be built on and the house has neither water nor electricity."

"Does that matter – all you need is a chaise longue!"

"I haven't accepted his gift yet."

"If I were you I would call this lawyer at once."

"To say what?"

Hubert pondered before replying:

"Start off by telling him you love him, then once that has sunk in, tell him that you are delighted to accept the gift from your father."

Mathilde lowered her eyes: "You're crazy. What make you think I've fallen in love with him?"

"Everything you have been trying not very successfully to hide, but which shows in your eyes, your every gesture and your flushed cheeks! And I don't believe that unflattering description of him for an instant."

She toyed nervously with her spoon.

"I'm right, aren't I?" he pursued.

"Hubert, you are so young..."

"I've had a lot of experience with the female sex. Talking of which, I must go. Francesca is waiting for me. By the way she'd like to meet you one day."

"How much do I owe you?"

"You owe me nothing at all, it was just a friendly chat. You could maybe book me a chaise longue at your farmhouse. Or maybe two - Francesca loves the sun."

"Give me a moment," said Mathilde nervously, "I have a question for you."

"Yes?"

"The other evening at my place you looked startled when you saw that photo on my bookshelf. You know Christophe don't you?"

"Not at all. For an instant I thought I recognised him, but I was mistaken."

He leaned towards her and put his hand on her shoulder.

"Promise you will call the lawyer as soon as I leave?"

"I promise."

"See you soon Mathilde. Take care."

Mathilde left and for a while wandered round Saint-Germain-des-Prés church, then sat down on a bench in the square to call the lawyer's office. Véronique's cheerful voice came on the phone.

"Sorry - Olivier doesn't work on Saturday afternoons."

"Ah!"

"If it's really urgent, I can give him a message and ask him to call you back."

"It's about my dossier…"

"So I would imagine."

"I have a few questions to put to him."

"I'll call him at once on his mobile. He usually responds promptly. Are you in Paris?"

"Yes."

"Very well, you can rely on me. Goodbye Miss Germain."

Five minutes later, Olivier called. His charming voice made Mathilde's heart race.

"Did you get back all right?" he asked soberly.

"Yes."

"It appears you have some questions."

"No, well, yes..."

"Send them to me by email and I will reply on Monday."

"Olivier, I..."

"I can't hear you very well. Where are you?"

"On a bench in Saint-Germain-des-Prés."

"I can hear the church bells ringing."

His tone had softened.

She relaxed:

"I can hear cicadas....where are YOU?"

"In my olive grove. Wait a minute, close your eyes and listen to this cicada – it's trying to tell you something. Can you hear it?"

"I don't understand what it's saying - perhaps you could translate..."

"It said that only one thing is missing for this to be the perfect place for me."

"And what's that?"

"Can't you guess?"

"I'm afraid I might guess wrong."

"Your presence."

A lump came to her throat and her eyes filled with tears.

"Why don't you answer, Mathilde? Why did you leave Aix without telling me?"

"It was on an impulse, after what happened last night, I..."

"Frédéric and I had an adult discussion about it all."

"But why didn't you call me?"

"I was waiting for you to make a move, I felt it was up to you. And as you have probably noticed I'm a bit shy and not very comfortable with women."

"I love you Olivier," she whispered just as a police car drove by, siren blaring.

"Mathilde, what was that? I didn't hear. I'm half deaf as well as half blind! Is that you laughing? But it's true - you shouldn't make fun of the disabled!"

"I'm not making fun of you, seriously," she giggled.

"I love hearing you laugh. You should do it more often.

"Olivier, I... David Stevenson is indeed my father. My mother confirmed it."

There was a pause. She held her breath till he spoke.

"I have an appointment in Paris in three days. Will you be around?"

"Yes."

"In that case we could meet to discuss....the next step with this dossier."

"As you wish, Sir."

"See you soon, Miss Germain."

"See you soon Olivier!"

Mathilde lingered on the bench dwelling on the prospect, then headed back along the Rue des Saints-Pères. She flew over the Seine, down the Grand Boulevards towards *Notre-Dame-de-Lorette* church and up the *Rue des Martyrs*. She felt as if she had wings. Paris had never seemed more beautiful or the air lovelier. She was longing to show it all to her newfound love.

On Monday, back at the office Benoît immediately asked her how her weekend went.

"You could have called me," he protested, "I tried to reach you but got no answer."

"I was very busy."

"I'm not surprised."

Mathilde went through her mail, taking a perverse pleasure in keeping her colleague on tenterhooks.

"Don't you want to tell me more?"

"You were not wrong when you guessed I might be inheriting some property."

"Ah, so my legendary flair is still intact!"

"There are a few discrepancies though."

"Tell me everything. I'm burning with curiosity!"

"It's a gift, but not from an old aunt - from an unknown American."

"Incredible!"

"And then, rather than a vineyard it's a patch of dry land with an old fig tree in it which no longer produces fruit, and a sort of shack with no mod cons."

"But why would an American you've never met donate this to you?"

"Fancy a coffee from the machine?" asked Mathilde meaningfully.

Benoît followed her into the corridor.

"The American is my biological father, something we were both unaware of until recently. My mother concealed the fact from the start, telling only her husband. I won't go into the details."

"You amaze me, sweetheart. You tell me all this unemotionally, as if you were not concerned."

"I'vc lcft out thc main bit though."

"I'm all ears."

"Its location is exceptional, at the foot of Mont Sainte-Victoire. You'd love it."

"When are you moving in?"

"I haven't officially accepted it yet. I've no idea how much it would cost and I probably can't afford the upkeep of a place like that. It's in a conservation area. I've got some details to sort out with the lawyer."

"What is Mr d'Estrello like, by the way?"

"You almost disappointed me, dear colleague. That's the first question you should have asked, and the most interesting one in my opinion."

"Does he have a beard? Is he bald? Does he have a paunch?"

"He's gorgeous if you want to know. In his early thirties, with dark hair and blue eyes. Of average height, but the lucky owner of a red Porsche."

How easy it is to doctor the truth to avoid hurting those you love!

"So basically, you didn't fancy him."

"Not really."

Benoît let out a jubilant cry.

"Whew, it was a close thing. I can now admit that I got a little worried when I saw you didn't want to be reached on the phone."

"There was no reason, I assure you."

"So much the better. I don't want you to leave - and I speak as a colleague and friend."

"Don't worry, it won't happen. I love Paris too much and I hate the heat, and all that blue sky stresses me out. Don't laugh, it's true!"

CHAPTER 8

Rendezvous in the Hotel Bristol

Three days later Olivier arrived in Paris. He stayed at the prestigious Hotel Bristol in the Rue du Faubourg Saint-Honoré, where Mathilde sometimes attended press conferences.

Over the phone he told her that it was a traditional family venue - his father used to stay there when on business in the capital, and his brother too. They got preferential rates. He would have preferred a more modest hotel for their meeting. Luxurious hotels intimidated him and made him feel uncomfortable. Mathilde stopped him, saying there was no need to justify his choice and that the hotel gardens were a haven of greenery and freshness in the middle of Paris, perfect for lunch during a heatwave. If you listened hard you could even hear birdsong, and, she added, there may even be olive trees in tubs on the terrace.

Seated at a table, Mathilde was wearing the same dress and shoes as on that first evening in Aix.

Her long hair hung loose over her shoulders. Olivier gazed at her appreciatively, which made her feel beautiful (further endorsed by discreet glances from businessmen at nearby tables).

Seeing Olivier again, waiting for her concealed behind a newspaper in the hotel lobby, brought tears to her eyes. Her heart raced, confirming Hubert's intuition. Yes, she was in love with this man she had only just met. In jeans, an open-necked white shirt and a lightweight jacket, he looked more at ease than in a suit. The first thing she noticed, however, was that he had changed his glasses. The new, almost invisible frames accentuated his dark eyes.

The waiter slipped Mathilde a menu with no pricelist. She studied it absorbedly. Olivier did not even look at his. He fidgeted on the garden chair which creaked under his weight. Unable to contain himself he leant towards her.

"Have you not noticed something different?" He glanced at her anxiously, seeking her approval.

"Yes," replied Mathilde distractedly. "Your glasses."

She looked up and stared at him.

"I'm tempted by the *tomato carpaccio with olive oil from Tuscany*. I wonder if their products are organic? The menu doesn't say."

He scowled: "Don't you like them? The optician said they suited me. She also mentioned that my eyesight could be corrected with contact lenses. But I look a bit less ridiculous already, don't I?"

Mathilde smiled.

"Now you look like a proper lawyer, Mr d'Estrello."

"That's what I am."

"In your spare time."

He put his hand over hers.

"Be sincere, Mathilde. Do you like me in my new glasses or not?"

"You shouldn't have gone to all that trouble for me," she mimicked his previous remark. "But yes, and I like you very much, Olivier, with or without your glasses."

He visibly relaxed. They ordered a light lunch and he chose a white Cassis wine. As the waiters moved discreetly around them, Mathilde told him everything she had learnt about her origins. He looked stunned.

"What have you decided then?"

"Regarding the house, nothing yet. That's more of a financial decision. I've drafted a whole list of questions for you. But as for David Stevenson, I keep wondering whether I really want to meet him. And that's only if he wants to meet ME - something I'm not even sure of."

"I hope I don't disappoint you, Mathilde, but I have to admit that when he came to my office in Aix he left no instructions to that effect and nothing in his manner indicated what his intentions were."

"What would you do in my place?"

"I'm not in a position to answer. My role is limited to the legal aspect of the donation. I have no mandate to take things any further."

"I'm not asking you as a lawyer," replied Mathilde, picking at her bread roll.

"From our conversation, Mr Stevenson seemed a decent sort of man."

"Olivier, I can't cope with all this on my own. I need your help."

"I promise I'll do all I can," he answered, pressing Mathilde's hand which he still cradled in his own.

Her attention was suddenly distracted. A couple had arrived at the far end of the terrace. Hubert, sporting a pair of Ray Bans and looking like a male model, was escorting a magnificent fifty-something woman oozing wealth and confidence. Christophe's ghost, which had hardly bothered her since her trip to the South of France, reappeared. She was very hurt when Hubert, removing his sunglasses, indicated to her in a brief impassive glance that they weren't meant to know each other. Mathilde shivered.

"You're cold!" said Olivier who missed nothing.

"Excuse me, I'll be back in a minute."

She walked calmly towards the hotel interior, making sure she passed Hubert's table.

A second later he joined her in a dim corner of the lobby.

"I've only got a few seconds. As you saw, I'm at work and my time is precious. I noticed you're with a gentleman. Is it your lawyer?"

She nodded.

"He looks very personable and has a nice physique. But I don't think he's the type to take advantage of it. He looks like the gentle sort. You have nothing to fear from such a man, Mathilde. I approve your choice. Go for it! Now I must leave you. My excuse of needing cigarettes is running out. Don't forget to check your hair and make-up before you go back to him."

He turned to go, then hesitated.

"I lied to you the other day. I often see Christophe in a bar in the Marais district, where I go with one of my regulars. He is always with the same guy. They seem very close. You should call it a day, Mathilde. He did the right thing - you couldn't have handled his admission."

She had to lean against a marble column to steady herself.

In the washroom she tried to regain her composure.

When she eventually returned to the table, Olivier's concerned expression transformed into delighted smile

"I thought I'd lost you again!"

She smiled weakly.

"Are you all right Mathilde? You're shaking."

"Everything's fine! I'm just a bit dizzy, that Cassis wine was simply delicious!"

The waiter appeared with the dessert menu. She waved him away.

"What about going up to your room?"

Olivier looked stupefied.

"Right now?"

"Don't you want to?"

"But... of course."

"Let's go then."

Embarrassed, he signalled the waiter who hurried up with the bill and a pen. Mathilde watched him sign. His hand was steady, his face as calm as usual. She, however, boiled with indignation, rage and longing to be made love to by someone who found her beautiful and an object of desire. She wanted him to explore every nook and cranny of her body with his hands and mouth. She wanted to feel his erection pressing against her stomach. She longed to feel him inside her, absorb him, and hear him groan in ecstasy and cry out as he climaxed.

Holding hands they headed for the lift. By chance nobody else was inside. Mathilde pressed herself against him. It was patently obvious that Olivier desired her. Her mood softened, she rested her forehead against his chest, feeling his rapid heartbeat. With one arm round her waist, he held her neck delicately in the other hand as if it was some fragile, precious object. His fingers sent a shiver down her spine. When she finally found the courage to look at him she saw his brown eyes burning with desire and she found him irresistibly attractive.

The lift came to a smooth stop and the bell sounded. Olivier fumbled with the bedroom door but finally managed to open it. The room exuded harmony and discreet luxury. He flung his jacket onto the bed.

Impatient, Mathilde joined him. She stretched up to hold his neck and draw his face closer to hers. *Please kiss me – now!* She pressed her lips against his, inserted her tongue and started to unbutton his shirt. Olivier with feverish fingers pulled back the straps on her dress to reveal her lacey bra.

Mathilde drew back and looked at him. He seemed as entranced as the first time they met. She wanted to savour every moment of his silent adoration.

She seized his hands and placed them on her breasts. Her nipples hardened almost painfully even before he caressed her. Why was he taking so long to undress her and caress her breasts with his tongue and lips? She had been waiting so long for this!

Instead of unfastening her bra, Olivier's fingers slid up her neck and into her hair like a comb, while the other hand ventured under her dress and crept up her thigh. Mathilde tilted her head backwards, lips parted, eyes wide - and waited. But nothing happened!

Olivier had stopped touching her and stood gazing at her as if in alarm. She clung to him, but he gently pushed her away then went over to the window.

"What's wrong?" she managed to blurt out.

"I think we're heading for a disaster, "he said, not turning round, "It would be better to stop here. I was mistaken."

"Are you no longer attracted by me?"

"I've dreamed of kissing you from the moment your lovely figure appeared at the door of my dark office. That's not the issue."

"I don't understand," she stammered.

He whirled round to face her.

"You are not here in this room for the right reasons, Mathilde. Or at least for the reasons I was hoping for. You're just using me to prove your seductive powers, that's all."

"Olivier, that's not true!" she sobbed.

"Don't try to deny it. I'm no Don Juan and my experience with women is admittedly somewhat limited but I know when someone is genuinely in love."

She took a few timid steps towards him.

"I love you, Olivier."

"Not the way I want," he said, slowly buttoning up his shirt.

"Then please explain."

The tears were now coursing down her cheeks, although she was beyond attempting to win him round.

"You've offered your body, Mathilde, but not your heart. I need both. It's as simple as that. It would be better if you left at once."

She backed towards the door slowly, adjusting her dress, hoping till the last minute that he would stop her but he didn't move. His face registered only sadness and disappointment.

“I’ve made you a promise and I’ll stick to it. But don’t expect anything more from me.”

Mathilde tottered out of the room on her high heels, forgetting to close the door. The lift was still at their floor. She stumbled inside, overwhelmed with grief.

CHAPTER 9

A Heart in Mourning

During the following days Mathilde applied what she called her *Heartbreak Quickfix Plan,* bitterly acknowledging that it had been much used. It was simple: stay as long as possible in the office and go out as much as possible with friends to avoid being alone. If she still felt miserable, she compensated by gorging herself on chocolate eclairs and buying outrageous shoes she knew she would never wear. One look at the shoe boxes piled inside her wardrobe showed how unsuccessful her love life had been so far.

Her last stratagem involved running down the person responsible for her misery. This method eventually worked in the case of Christophe. With Olivier she thought it would be easy. He had landed in her life by chance when she was vulnerable and ready to accept anyone. How could she have let herself fall into the trap? This man was nothing like her usual type. On top of his physical shortcomings, of which he made no secret, he was old-fashioned, hyper-sensitive, one-track, provincial, etc. She forced herself to a conclusion: *I don't love him, full stop. It's just as well he rejected me.*

The only thing was that her plan didn't work. Mattie balked at being fooled by Mathilde. At night she stifled her cries in her pillow: *I love you Olivier, you're the man of my dreams. Why did you reject me too? How can I get you back?*

A week had passed since the painful episode at the Hotel Bristol. Paris was starting to put up decorations for the 14th July celebrations and rain was forecast. A heart in mourning would have trouble coping with all the fanfare. The capital emptied itself of its residents, to be replaced by hordes of noisy tourists. The city felt no longer hers and she was upset to see her friends leaving one after the other. Hubert could not be contacted, his voicemail indicating that he had flown off to the Caribbean.

In the office Benoît observed her but said nothing, trying to conceal his concern. He knew her too well to force it out of her. He just had to wait for her to open up, reassuring her that he was there for her, like a caring big brother. He had given up on being anything more. Beautiful Mathilde would never be his.

One Friday evening, though, she agreed to have dinner with him in the Lebanese restaurant he kept going on about. As she walked up to their table he was surprised to see that she had made an effort with her appearance. She wore a white almost transparent shirt over loose black pants, her waist accentuated by a wide black leather belt adorned with gold lion heads with large rings in their mouths. Her blond hair was swept back into a low loose chignon. Her made-up eyes and rouged lips glittered strangely. Benoît had trouble recognising his friend, but she was attracting all the male glances.

"Good evening, my lovely," he greeted her as she sat down opposite him, "You look dazzling, and I'm flattered. Your belt is begging me to attach a chain to it, make you my slave and drag you out of here - too many eyes are ogling you."

Mathilde leant forward: "It's Hermès, a little something I've just treated myself to."

"Hard to wear in a *provençal* house with no mod cons!"

Mathilde looked around for something to throw at him. But Benoît had already moved the salt cellar out of reach and was holding onto the breadbasket.

They ordered mezze, an assortment of kebabs and Lebanese wine. A basket of warm flatbread arrived.

Mathilde devoured it with the humous and the aubergine caviar, emptied her glass and held it out to Benoît for more.

"I've hardly ever seen you eat and drink so furiously," he said in astonishment, as he reached out for the bottle, "What's wrong?"

She made a vague gesture in reply.

"You can tell a woman in love by her lack of appetite," he added, "So you're not in love, unless you have been disappointed, really disappointed (and I'm guessing that's it)."

She merely shrugged: "That's irrelevant, I'm hungry that's all, and stop analysing my every gesture!"

"Very well then, *Mademoiselle*. What would you like us to talk about?"

"About you, for once. Your love life, for example."

"I love my son, Spain, my work, wine, cigarettes..."

"I know all that. You're forgetting women, that's what interests me."

"There's nothing exciting to recount. It's been dead calm since my divorce. I'm waiting till Pablo grows up. For the moment I have him with me for as long as I'm allowed."

"Your son is an alibi for your solitude. If you want to move on, I know plenty intelligent, sexy, single girlfriends who are looking for love. There's one called Julie – she's a smart cookie, Spanish looking. You'd get on really well."

"Don't bother playing at go-between, Mattie. My heart is taken by a tall blonde. Not even a smart brunette can get a look in."

"Hey, stop that. Don't look at me with that lovelorn expression; You know full well that..."

"That I'm not your type. I know, I know. Forget it... I'd be delighted to meet this Julie. Happy now?"

"Yes. Let's drink to your wise decision. Is there any wine left?"

Benoît lifted the bottle to check.

"Just a drop – and it's all for you. Which means you'll be married by the end of the year."

"Don't talk rubbish."

When they left the restaurant it was pouring rain and a storm was brewing. Benoît took off his jacket and put it over Mathilde's shoulders. In no time they were soaking and she started shivering. He noticed a hotel neon sign and pulled her under the porch. They sheltered there for a few minutes, while the rain fell even more heavily. Mathilde's teeth were chattering. Her thin shirt stuck to her skin, revealing her breasts and her nipples straining against her lacy brassiere.

"I'm freezing!" she said, nestling into Benoît's chest.

He took her hand and ushered her inside the hotel. Behind the plain wooden desk a man was dozing.

"We need a room with a bathroom" said Benoît placing a banknote on the counter.

The man turned and nonchalantly took a key from the rack.

"Room 7, it's our last room. Third floor on the left."

"This place is used by prostitutes!" giggled Mathilde in the lift.

"At least you'll be able to have a hot shower."

"I've always wanted to get inside a brothel, out of mere curiosity and also as a journalist, of course!"

"But of course! I hope the towels are dry. Let's start by drying your hair. Put on my shirt. We can call a taxi."

"Benoît, do you remember your proposal?"

"Which one?"

"*Wherever and whenever...*"

"No."

They paused outside Room 7.

"How come? There was a taxi rank at the end of the street!"

"By the time you were home you'd have caught your death of cold."

The room was exactly as Mathilde imagined – faded wallpaper, dated furniture, dim lighting, pink lampshades and a nasty smell. She felt sick.

Benoît had disappeared into the bathroom behind a thin wooden partition. He returned with a towel.

"They don't come any rougher," he joked.

Mathilde just stood there, aghast. He was making fun of her.

"Is your curiosity satisfied now? In case you want to know, there's a bidet through there. Come and get dry. You're still shivering."

He pushed her onto the bed, untied her hair and gently dried it. Dazed by the alcohol and the incongruous situation Mathilde let it happen. Benoît dropped the towel, seized her face and brought his lips towards hers. She shut her eyes. In her imagination she saw Olivier walking calmly towards her, while she ran into his waiting arms. *I love him!*

"I love him."

Benoît drew back, startled.

"What's that?"

"I love him, Benoît, I love him, I'm sorry..."

"Who?"

"My lawyer."

He tried to put on a brave face.

"I should have suspected something when you said you didn't fancy him. Women often think the opposite of what they say when it comes to love."

"Well, then at least there's nothing to regret. And thanks to me you know what a brothel looks like. As you can see it's not up to much."

She stroked his cheek.

"I'll get over it, don't worry" he said.

He went to the window and looked out.

"The storm has passed. There are plenty taxis waiting. You'll be home in ten minutes. I won't be seeing you till Monday. Off you go, darling. I'll take advantage of this room and rest a bit. I'm dog tired."

"Don't you want me to stay a little longer?" she asked, concerned.

"No way. Off you go. It's better that way. Perhaps one day I'll thank your lawyer for having unintentionally preserved a friendship that I was stupidly about to spoil."

CHAPTER 10

The daughter of two fathers

The next morning Mathilde flew to Nice to see her mother. They headed to the *Cours Saleya* and sat in the sunshine at a pavement café. The flower market was in full swing.

Mathilde showed her mother the photo she had found at the *Mas du Figuier*. Micheline studied it, clearly moved.

"You know, darling, the weeks I spent at the house with David were magic. I hope you get to experience such moments of happiness yourself."

"Mother, you've told me nothing about your affair. I don't understand – you were MARRIED!"

"We had decided to separate for a while to think things over. We were having trouble starting a family and our relationship was under strain."

The waiter brought them some barley water. Micheline sipped hers for several moments before continuing:

"I decided to have a break at my cousin's place in Aix. By sheer chance I met this charming American at the *Deux Garçons* in the Cours Mirabeau. He was irresistible with his blond hair and charming accent. I was exactly the age you are today, dear Mathilde. I had dark hair at the time and wasn't too bad looking. Very French looking, he said that day, which for an American, you know, is a real compliment. He told me that he was staying in France for artistic reasons. He had just finished his degree in History of Art and was obsessed with Cézanne's paintings. A travel agent had asked him to organise a programme of cultural visits on Cézanne. Did you know that it's American money that saved Cézanne's studio in Aix? That's where we kissed for the first time, and where something dramatic almost happened."

She stopped. Mathilde was touched to see her mother's nostalgic smile. She had never ever opened up to her like that before.

"A drama?!"

"In a moment of passion, David bumped into the *nature morte* table and a jug started to roll off. He caught it before it fell, but only just! We had a really great time together. He had rented the farm house because of its perfect location. We spent hours gazing at the effect of the light on the slopes of *Mont Sainte-*

Victoire. It was October but still warm. In the evening David used to light the fire and we would talk or read for hours before going to bed. He was very cultured. He opened up new horizons for me. He was an amateur painter and did my portrait there so he could have a souvenir of me, he said. On his last day I accompanied him to Orly airport and just before we separated he asked me to join him in the States. He wanted to marry me. I hadn't told him I was already married. And you know the rest. Do remember one thing, dear Mathilde – you are a child born from love, and the daughter of two fathers."

Mathilde was relieved she could hide the turmoil she felt behind her sunglasses. Once they had both recovered their composure, she decided to break her news.

"I've asked the lawyer to get in touch with David Stevenson on my behalf and say I would like to meet him."

Micheline clasped her daughter's hand.

"You have done the right thing, my dear," she said in a tremulous voice.

They stayed silent for a moment, closer than they had ever been.

"Mother, I think I'm in love," Mathilde blurted, "And his name is Olivier."

“Are you in love, or do you really and truly love him?”

“I really love him.”

“And Olivier?”

Mathilde’s face clouded over.

“I was clumsy. We have split up on a misunderstanding.”

“If he means a lot to you it’s up to you to make a move. Don’t give up my dear. You should never let True Love pass you by.”

CHAPTER 11

An Unexpected Visitor

Mathilde returned to Paris reassured, but unsure as to how to win back Olivier. The simplest thing would be to call him and simply tell him about her recent doomed love affair - he would probably understand. But she lacked the courage. Even mentioning Christophe was still beyond her.

On the Monday morning after the editorial meeting Benoît asked her about her holiday plans.

"I have to arrange the schedule. What dates do you want?"

"I don't mind, I have nothing organised."

He looked astonished: "Not going down to Provence?"

"No plans at all," she replied moodily.

"I was wondering why you looked so pasty faced. Well, why not pick a nice sunny destination? Book yourself into a holiday club or something with your girlfriends."

"It so happens my friends have gone ahead with their own plans."

"Poor Mathilde, left behind all alone!" he teased.

"Drop it, you can't help. Why don't you take time off first - I may be pale but look at yourself. You're positively GREEN!"

"Mattie, you know perfectly well I don't have my son with me till August."

"In that case, why ask me?"

"Because I have to be your boss right till the end."

"You irritate me."

Fortunately just then she got a call from reception.

"Yes, Claire...Who?! Mr d'Estrello?! I'll be right down. Don't let him get away, whatever you do. Tell him I'm coming."

She knocked over her chair in her haste, amusing Benoît.

"Don't let him get away whatever you do!" he mimicked, "Since when do our visitors want to run away? This newspaper office isn't a prison or a zoo!"

He ducked under his desk to avoid the box of paperclips which landed on Odile's desk two rows away and burst open.

"It'll be mayhem," predicted Benoît.

But Mathilde was already gone. She ignored the lift and flew down the stairs, her heart pounding.

However the figure waiting at the reception desk was not Olivier.

"I'm really sorry to disappoint you," said Frédéric coming to meet her, "I know you'd rather see my brother, but as you can imagine, I'm not all that happy to be here myself.

He looked genuinely embarrassed in front of a silent, hostile Mathilde.

"What's the purpose of your visit? We are in the middle of finalising today's edition. I don't have much time."

"It won't take long, but I'd rather talk somewhere private..."

"The café next door is noisy enough, nobody will hear our conversation."

"Show me the way."

They left hurriedly, Mathilde leading the way. They sat at the bar inside the café.

"Hello, *Mademoiselle!*" proclaimed the owner on seeing them, "We haven't seen you for a while. What'll it be?"

"I'll have a mint cordial, please."

"Make it two," said Frédéric, grimacing slightly.

"So, Mr d'Estrello, what is this all about?"

"I'm passing through Paris and I wanted to take the opportunity to tell you that Olivier has finalised your dossier. You can imagine that when he asked me to give you the message I told him to get lost. We are hot-blooded down in the South of France. We almost came to blows. Anyway, so as not to make things worse, I finally accepted to pass on the message, although inheritance, legacies, donations, etc. are not my line of business."

Mathilde twiddled with her wristwatch. Frédéric put the file on the counter and patted it nervously.

"Out of a sense of duty, I leafed through it. My brother has answered all your legal and technical queries with his usual precision and thoroughness. Plus, I have to tell you that, as you requested, he contacted Mr Stevenson and has convinced him to meet you. You just have to name the date and the place."

"A cognac please and make it quick!" cried Mathilde.

"Make it two!" chimed Frédéric.

"I'm so pleased!

He did that for me. He kept his word. She hid her face in her hands to hide her emotion:

"Frankly, I'd rather he told you directly. My brother is a total fool, despite being the cleverest one in the family."

Mathilde smiled into her glass.

"You mustn't laugh. I don't know what you've done to him, Mathilde, but he's unhappy. And because I feel that I owe you both following that disastrous evening at the Festival, the main reason I've come here is to tell you this. Nobody knows Olivier like I do. Admittedly we are not alike, we don't have the same tastes, we've fought non-stop since we were kids, but we are very close. My brother deserves to find love but so far he's not had much luck with women. They tend to take advantage of his kindness and generosity. Mathilde, you really must do something. I can't bear seeing him this way."

"He rejected me," she replied, her laughter turning to tears, "It's always the same with me. I scare men away. What can I do about it?"

"Go and find him. He loves you and he's waiting for you, I swear he is."

"How can you be so sure?"

"Because of this!"

He brandished a sheet of paper from the folder.

"This headed paper from the *Bastide de l'Ange* was in the wrong file. But as I've said, my brother is the meticulous sort so it wasn't in there by chance. Or else it's a Freudian slip on his part. Which boils down to the same thing."

Mathilde seized it. There was nothing written on it.

"The *Bastide de l'Ange*?"

"Did he never mention it to you? It's the family property outside Aix. When our father dies it will go to Olivier but he already considers it his. He is very attached to the place. There's no way would I have wanted it."

"But there's nothing written on it!" she cried, waving the sheet at him.

"That blank sheet says more than words, don't you think? Olivier hardly ever leaves his beloved country residence. He's there now. The next move is up to you."

"Are you sure he's expecting me?"

"Mathilde, if that wasn't the case I'd have no reason to be here. I give you my word. Must I personally drag you to the station? Or maybe you'd rather travel in my Porsche, which I doubt."

She smiled: "I'd rather go by train."

Frédéric raised his glass: "To Love!"

Back in the office Mathilde jubilantly announced to her boss that she would be on holiday the next day, taking off the whole five weeks she was entitled to.

"I'll put that down, it's no problem," he said.

She passed behind his chair, put her arms round his neck and pressed her cheek against his.

"I adore you. And I always will."

He smiled valiantly.

"Off you go, darling. Enjoy yourself in Provence but don't forget to come back. In the meantime, if I were you, I'd go and apologise to Odile."

"Never!" she whispered into his ear.

Benoît watched her leave the office, feeling he might never see her again, his heart gripped in a vice. He felt suffocated.

CHAPTER 12

The Bastide de l'Ange

At Aix train station the taxi driver put on his glasses to examine the paper handed to him by his passenger.

"The *Bastide de l'Ange*! I know it well, no need for the map. The d'Estrello son lives there, the elder one. He's taken over the family property. Jolly brave, I'd say. It's a nice place. Do you know it?"

"No."

"You'll see for yourself then."

He started the engine and turned to look at her.

"Off we go. Sit back and relax, *Mademoiselle.*"

His passenger made no reply. After a while he couldn't resist starting up the conversation again.

"Are you here on business?"

"Yes, in a way..."

"I must say you are not the talkative sort. Are you from Paris?"

"Yes."

"Mind you, I should have guessed, you have that clipped accent!"

Mathilde burst out laughing.

"There – how nice to hear a pretty girl laugh! Here in the South of France we tend to be talkative. So, you know d'Estrello then?"

"Just a little."

"He's a good guy. I knew him as a kid. He's got crazy ideas though. I don't know if it's because of his name, but he got hold of the idea of producing olive oil again on the estate. He won't make a fortune out of it, poor chap, but if that's what he likes doing.... He should have become a farmer not a lawyer. And what do you do for a living?"

"I'm a journalist."

"I'd never have guessed – you're not exactly inquisitive!"

"I'm on holiday."

"Here we are! See the row of plane trees over there? The house is at the end of the lane."

The taxi drove past the massive trees, their trunks patched brown, grey and yellow and peeling in places.

"Lovely, aren't they?" continued the driver, "Nothing like your shrivelled old Paris specimens!"

But Mathilde had only eyes for the house. Higher than it was wide, its small-paned windows symmetrically punctuated the pink stucco facade. She felt as if she had always known this place. It seemed to her that she had arrived at a point to which all her past experiences, including her failures, had inevitably been leading. She was grateful to the driver for letting her indulge her emotions in silence.

The car drove round a fountain adorned with a smiling cherub and pulled up at the foot of the shallow front steps. Two large glazed tubs of oleander framed the arched french windows, one of which stood wide open, inviting her to enter. She could see the Provence countryside through the far end of the long corridor. Mathilde paid the taxi driver, knowing that next day the rumour would be going round that a Parisian journalist was involved with the Master of the House.

A woman in an apron appeared at the door. She greeted the visitor with a broad smile. "Welcome to the *Bastide de l'Ange!*"

"I'm Mathilde Germain."

I know that, said her twinkling eyes.

"I'm Hortense the housekeeper. Delighted to meet you. Olivier is out on the slopes. I'll tell him you've arrived. Come in and leave your bag."

Mathilde followed her along the terracotta tiled corridor and out onto the terrace which ran along the house. Climbing plants adorned the trellis and fragrant flowering shrubs stood in the row of tubs. Wrought iron tables and wicker chairs were set out along the terrace, and in the garden, beds of aromatic plants, edged with boxwood, lay round the fountain whose jets of water formed a corolla. And beyond that, cypress trees surrounded a stone bathing pool, the light reflecting in its green depths. A cat came up and rubbed against Mathilde's legs. She could hear a dog barking in the distance.

"He's coming," announced the housekeeper, slipping her phone back into her apron pocket.

"From which direction?" asked Mathilde in a trembling voice.

"Follow that path down to the right and you'll come to the olive grove. Go along the first row of trees on your left. You'll soon see him."

Mathilde hurried along the path, her heart pounding. She hoped she wouldn't miss him so that he could see how much she loved him, so that he could see that she was ready to give up her entire past life, to be born again in Provence, where she had been conceived. At last she saw his tall figure approaching, framed against the light. A golden labrador bounded along beside him.

On seeing Mathilde, Olivier stopped, called the dog back and gazed at her bathed in the golden glow of the late afternoon. The heat was less oppressive. A blend of thyme, mint and lavender filled the air. Insects scuttled as she went past. All her senses exulted in the magic of the moment. At times there was total silence, more intense than she had ever experienced. Then Nature's symphony started up again in the balmy air.

The man she loved was now walking towards her with his loose-limbed gait. As he got closer she impulsively started running towards him. He opened his arms and she fell against his chest, breathing in his scent while his lips caressed her blond hair.

"I was waiting for you," he said simply.

She drew back and cupped his face in her hand, laughing. He was wearing his old glasses.

"I broke my new ones," he admitted sheepishly.

"Just as well."

He hugged her then drew her face towards his. Just as they were about to exchange their first kiss, a shrill insect sound burst out above them. Mathilde started. More rasping calls started up further afield, the noise becoming deafening.

"Provence is welcoming you," smiled Olivier, "I hadn't expected the fanfare quite so early, but your cicada friends, including that noisy one up this tree, are telling you that everything is now in perfect harmony. And I'd like to add, so they can hear, that they'll have to stop rubbing their wings when I'm trying to kiss the woman I love."

He picked Mathilde up in his arms.

"Let's sneak off to a quieter spot."

They crossed the olive grove made their way to the terrace, inside the house and upstairs. The master bedroom was at the end of a long corridor. The wooden shutters were closed, shafts of light piercing the dim interior. Olivier laid her on the bed, its counterpane neatly folded back. He sat down beside her and simply looked at her, savouring that special moment which precedes the first time. Under his loving gaze Mathilde sensed a growing impatience. She felt as if she was a continent that he was about to explore and conquer. A clock solemnly struck the hour somewhere in the house. Time stopped for them that sweet July afternoon. Behind the closed shutters she could still feel the powerful presence of Nature with the buzzing of insects, the singing of birds, the rustling of the wind in the trees as well and the distant rumble of an engine. To this was added the thudding heartbeat of the man she loved as he bent over her.

He slowly slid down her dress straps, waiting till the last moment to embrace her, as if still seeking reassurance before embarking on his exploration, checking the terrain.

"Let's pick up where we left off," he said with a smile.

Mathilde lowered her eyes. He kissed her lightly on the shoulder.

"I apologise for having doubted your love. That palatial bedroom intimidated me."

"Shh", she said, removing his glasses.

"Now I'm deprived of the pleasure of seeing you," he said sadly.

"Your hands will see me."

She placed his hands on her breasts, offering him the first contours of the continent he was about to explore – and conquer more inquisitively, respectfully and tenderly than any other lover, and one she wanted never to leave her shores.

Their faces almost touched. Mathilde's head spun under Olivier's loving gaze. She closed her eyes. His soft lips came into contact with hers. She remembered that first time in his office, when she noticed the sensual mouth which was now savouring hers. His tongue played with hers, arousing her palate and thrilling her inside. Her whole body came alive, taut with desire. Her dress slid to the floor. Olivier's hands trembled as he removed her brassiere. Mathilde caressed his muscular chest under his shirt, tugging at the buttons, longing to feel it against her breasts. She had never desired anyone like this. He whispered words of love in French and Italian, as seductively as that first time she heard his voice on the phone.

At last they were naked. He stopped caressing her to look at her, his eyes moist.

"I've been waiting for you for so long."

"It's been a long journey for me too, dearest love. But I know I've reached my destination."

Mathilde stroked his eyelids and cheeks. Overcome with emotion, he hid his face in her mass of blond hair.

"Come here," he murmured.

He lay back and drew her towards him. Slowly, artfully, taking his time, he took possession of her waiting body and she knew then that her intuitions had been right.

Later, as they rose, a smell of apricot tart wafted up from the kitchen and a stray dove cooed on the window ledge outside.

Olivier, full of newfound energy, announced: "Rest now, my love. I'm off for a swim."

CHAPTER 13

Scents of the Garrigue

The scent of the *garrigue* wafted into the large kitchen, Hortense's personal domain. With its red tiles, ancient wood stove, bread bin and stone sink, it was an authentic *provençal* kitchen which Olivier clearly had no intention of modernising. Leaning over Hortense's shoulder, he sniffed the dish she had just removed from the oven.

"Courgette and tomato gratin from the garden with a touch of olive oil from the *Bastide de l'Ange*," announced Hortense proudly to Mathilde who was lingering at the door enjoying the spectacle of her tall man in his bathrobe cuddling the little aproned lady who had been his nanny.

"Hortense is the best cook for miles around," declared the Master of the House.

"Come on, no flattery please, dear. With produce like yours cooking is child's play!"

She looked delighted, though. Olivier twirled her round in his arms.

"Slow down, you'll make me dizzy! Put me down, please! *Mademoiselle*, what have you done to him, to put him in such a mood?!"

She smiled at Mathilde. Olivier gently put Hortense down, then crossed over to Mathilde and put his arm round her waist.

"What she has done is love me, this young lady with the sweet name of Mathilde," he replied, exaggerating his *provençal* accent.

Hortense blushed.

"That stove gets so hot," she quickly said, "Give me a few minutes for the shoulder of lamb, and dinner will be ready. I've laid the table on the terrace. You'll be fine out there. The wine is in a cooler. I don't think I've forgotten anything. Oh, and the apricot tart is waiting in the oven."

She undid her apron.

"I'll be off now, my children. Good night and see you tomorrow."

"Thank you for this veritable feast, Hortense. Have a safe trip home," said Olivier.

He kissed Mathilde on the neck.

"I'll dash upstairs and get dressed. I won't be long."

Mathilde left the kitchen which opened onto a covered terrace. It was not yet dark but the first stars already shone palely in the sky as dusk approached. Some lights twinkled far off in the neighbouring hills. The air was still thick with the scents of the day released by the heat. The shrill noise of the cicadas faded then returned in ever more deafening waves, but the evening ritual was soon to cease.

She lit the tealights she found on the table. The sight of Olivier hurrying down the steps sent a sharp charge of emotion through her. He had combed his hair off his face and his blue shirt with its rolled-up sleeves revealed a glimpse of his chest. He wore cotton trousers and he had bare feet inside his worn suede moccasins. She drank in the sight of him, absorbed his presence.

"What's wrong with me?" he asked anxiously, removing his glasses.

"You're very handsome."

"You're the first woman to tell me that apart from Hortense when I was small and that doesn't count. Even my mother never found me handsome, she always compared me with Frédéric."

"You are much better looking than him," she said ruffling his dark hair.

He held her tight.

"Let's get the food," he said at length, "I'm starving."

He carved the meat, served her generously then poured out the rosé. They clinked their glasses.

"Do you remember our picnic at the house?"

"You talk as if we we've been together for years!" she smiled.

"I'll always remember it as vividly as I do today."

Perching his spectacles on his forehead he swirled his glass, admiring the colour of the wine.

She stroked his cheek.

"Your efforts to please me were very touching."

"I really wanted you to share my passion for this magical place. But as for pleasing you, I knew it was not going to be that easy."

"You were wrong. I fell in love with you and Mont Sainte-Victoire at the same time."

"Hardly surprising," he said proudly.

"You know something, when I was looking round the house on my own I came across a copy of *Travels with a Donkey in the Cévennes*."

"By Robert Louis Stevenson?"

"My mother made me read it when I was a child. She talked about it so emotionally that I felt it was not just the story that moved her, that there must have been another reason. Of course I was too young to imagine that..."

Tears sprang to Mathilde's eyes.

"Luckily for you I'm the old-fashioned type who has an impressive collection of large white handkerchiefs," said Olivier dabbing her cheeks.

She laughed through her tears: "Sorry!"

"There's no need to apologise, my darling. I understand the shock you must have had, I was prepared for it."

"You were perfect."

In the candlelight, they enjoyed the delicious meal prepared by Hortense. Olivier radiated happiness, pampering his companion and seeming to find her endlessly fascinating. Mathilde basked in his adoration. For the first time in her life she was at peace with herself and in tune with her surroundings, totally trusting the man who had just pleasured her body and who she knew she would love for a long time to come.

I have arrived. The Bastide de l'Ange had always been waiting for me.

A bat suddenly flew round their table out of the darkness and Mathilde gave a terrified cry. Olivier cradled her in his arms.

"Don't be scared. Bats are harmless. They live in an old building close by. Tomorrow I'll show you round the property and we can wake them while they are asleep. You'll learn to love them and find them beautiful despite their appearance."

A telephone rang somewhere in the house. With a sense of foreboding Mathilde jumped up:

"It's my phone – I left it inside."

She ran into the corridor. Her hands trembled as she rummaged through her bag.

"Hello?"

"It's Odile. I have bad news. Benoît has had a heart attack – a bad one."

Mathilde stifled a cry.

"He set off to cycle home and collapsed a few yards from the office. He's in intensive care. It seems to be touch and go. I have to let other people know so I'll hang up. Sorry to give you such bad news. I'll keep you posted."

Mathilde stood there stunned, clutching her phone. When Olivier came in he found her slumped against the wall sobbing into her hands. He crouched down beside her and waited till she could speak.

"Don't worry, I'm here," he said cradling her.

CHAPTER 14

The First Morning

They spent the night in each other's arms, exchanging soothing words and caresses, and only fell asleep around daybreak. Some time later a door slammed downstairs. Mathilde opened her eyes, feeling she was emerging from a nightmare but finding Olivier asleep beside her, one arm flung over her shoulder and a leg across her thigh, calmed her.

Nothing bad can happen to me while he is with me. He's my port in a storm.

A delicious smell of coffee and toast wafted up from the kitchen.

This is our first morning together.

Olivier sighed in his sleep and snuggled closer. She stroked his hair and neck, then abruptly checked herself. What right had she to think egoistically of her own happiness when her friend Benoît was fighting for his life in a hospital room?

She turned towards Olivier.

"Mathilde!" he cried, starting awake.

He reached out to the bedside table: “My glasses! What time is it?”

She restrained him, covered his chest with little nibbling kisses.

“Mathilde, what are you doing?”

“Shh! What I’m doing is loving you,” she said, mimicking his accent.

They made love slowly and tenderly, savouring each moment of pleasure as if it was for the last time.

“Love conquers all,” she said as, lying on their backs, they slowly returned to reality.

Olivier rose and opened the shutters. Light and heat poured into the room.

“Our first morning together,” he announced, filling his lungs with the morning air.

They were having breakfast in the kitchen when Odile called back. Olivier saw the relief on Mathilde’s face as she hung up.

“Benoît has got through the night but he’s still on a ventilator. The doctors think he’ll make it and that there will be no lasting effects.”

He hugged her as she cried and laughed at the same time.

“Do you want to go to Paris today?”

“He’s not allowed visitors at the moment.”

"Then come with me, darling, I've something to show you," he said, jumping up.

They headed for the olive grove, its slender trunks and thin low branches bearing pale greyish green olives barely visible among the leaves.

"Pruning olive trees is an art - the aim being to maximise the impact of the light through the branches," Olivier informed her a teacherly tone.

"Like Cézanne's art," smiled Mathilde.

"Almost. But then you also have to limit the height of the tree to make harvesting easier. I've learnt what I know from past generations of growers, but it's a constant learning curve. No matter how much care you put into it there are still good years and bad years. Climate doesn't explain it all either."

"I thought the trees would have thick gnarled trunks, but these are young."

"That's what I wanted to show you. Look carefully – every tree has thin trunks growing out of old stumps. In 1956 the frost killed most of the olive groves around here. They feared olive growing would be gone forever in Provence, but then, against all expectations, the next year everything came back to life. Shoots started to spring from the dead stumps. Life proves stronger than death."

Mathilde threw her arms round his neck.

"I never thought for a moment I'd fall head over heels in love with an old sage from Provence!"

"November is harvest time, then the olives go to the mill. In January I bottle the cold pressed oil from the *Bastide*. My production is still modest but I have great plans. I'd like to make the estate flourish like it did in the time of my great grandparents. And I'd love you to be there at my side. Don't say anything – I'm not asking you to give me an answer now. You have your career and your own dreams. But believe the words of an old sage when I say that every minute in life is precious and I'd like to spend as much of it as possible with you."

A week later they went up to Paris. Olivier accompanied Mathilde to Salpetriere hospital where she went to visit Benoît. She found him lying in bed attached to a drip and monitors. As chance would have it, Odile had turned up at the same time. They stared at each other warily from both sides of the bed.

"My heart attack has given me the chance to see my two best friends together at last," joked Benoît, "Why not shake hands and make peace? You cannot refuse a request from a man who has so narrowly escaped death."

Since neither moved, he took their hands and clasped them together on the bedsheet.

"The worst is over. Now I just need to see your two signatures on a ground-breaking article and I shall die happy."

They both cried out indignantly. A nurse popped her head round the door to say that visiting time was over. Odile beat a hasty retreat but Benoît held Mathilde back.

"You are transformed, Mattie. More beautiful than ever. The Provence climate suits you."

She kissed his forehead: "I'm just happy that you have pulled through."

"No need to pussyfoot with me. I've survived a heart attack and will be back to full strength soon. My heart can take anything. Is that lawyer of yours here?"

"He's waiting in the corridor."

"Please don't take advantage of my weak state. I glimpsed someone outside when the nurse came in – a tall well-built chap with large spectacles. If I remember correctly you mentioned a handsome man of average height!"

"Are you sure? I must have made a mistake."

"Mattie, I only hope he loves you as much as you deserve. If he harms even as much as a hair on your head I'll do him in. Tell him to come in so we can have it out straight away."

He slumped back onto his pillow.

“I’d like to, but there’s a nurse on duty outside. Once you’re fully recovered I’ll introduce you to Olivier and you’ll see you have no reason to worry.”

“You could at least tell him to change his spectacles.”

“See you soon, darling,” said Mathilde as she left.

CHAPTER 15

An American in Paris

David Stevenson returned to Paris at the beginning of August. Mathilde again broke off her holiday and travelled north.

Rather than meet at Charles de Gaulle airport, they had arranged to see each other at his hotel on the Left Bank among the antique shops and art galleries.

Olivier dropped Mathilde outside the hotel. She hesitated at the door:

"I'm scared."

He gave her a reassuring hug: "Don't worry, it'll be fine."

"Why don't you come with me!"

"No, it's not my place. It's a special occasion for the two of you. I'll see you this evening for dinner. Be brave, darling. You are about to experience one of the biggest moments in your life."

The American stood waiting at the reception desk. When he saw a tall young blonde who looked very like him enter the hotel, he approached with a welcoming smile and instantly dissolved all Mathilde's apprehensions. They didn't embrace or shake hands, but simply stood and contemplated each other.

"Where would you like us to go?" asked David.

"To Montmartre" replied Mathilde impulsively.

As they walked along the Rue des Saints-Pères, David reached for his daughter's arm as if it was the most natural thing in the world.

"Do you want me to use *vous* or *tu*? It's so much easier in English as we only have the one form of address, but with you French it's much more complicated."

"I'd rather the more formal *vous*" said Mathilde shyly.

"As you wish, *Mademoiselle*."

The funicular railway took them up to the *Sacré-Cœur* church.

"This is my first time in Montmartre. I've often come to Paris but never here."

David Stevenson spoke in quaint academic French with an adorable accent. Mathilde soon understood why her mother had fallen for this courteous, open-minded American who seemed touched to be meeting his daughter for the first time.

They sat down at a sidewalk café in the *Place du Tertre* and ordered peppermint cordial.

An artist came up and offered to sketch Mathilde.

"First show me what you do," said David, "I know a little about art."

The artist opened his portfolio.

"Not bad. All right, then. You can sketch my daughter while we are chatting but please don't disturb us. We have a lot to catch up on," he said, eyeing Mathilde.

He said 'my daughter' – just like that!

She fiddled with her glass and David watched her with a little smile.

"When your mother called to tell me out of the blue that I had a daughter in France I thought at first it was some kind of poor joke, an attempt at blackmail or whatever. I've been married for twenty-five years and have two kids. I am a Professor at the Washington University, a position of considerable standing. You know what Americans are like – unlike the French they are puritanical. I flatly refused to entertain the idea. She didn't insist."

Mathilde listened with rapt attention, forgetting about the artist at his easel.

"In the days that followed I kept thinking about it. I'd shoved our love affair back into the recesses of my memory but it kept resurfacing like a series of bubbles. I was extremely shaken. My wife noticed I was upset so I told her the whole story – the first time I had ever confided in anyone. It was she who convinced me to do something about it. Without her approval I wouldn't have made a move, at least I don't think so..."

Mathilde's face clouded.

"Don't move," said David, "I'll go and see how our artist is doing."

He returned to the table looking pleased.

"So I got back in touch with Micheline and we talked frankly. I understood then why she had refused to follow me to the States. Sometimes silence is better than the truth, Mathilde. Her decision was laudable, she loved her husband very much. I am sure now that we wouldn't have been very happy together in a country that was so foreign to her. But at the time I had no such doubts. What would I have done if I'd found out she was carrying our child? She didn't know she was pregnant when she accompanied me to Orly airport. Anyway, it's pointless trying to undo the past. There is nothing to regret. All that matters is the future, and here we are together today, sitting at a café in the Paris sunshine. It's all so wonderful and extraordinary that I can hardly believe it is happening."

The artist came up with the portrait. David paid and handed the charcoal sketch to Mathilde.

"What do you think of it? Original no?"

Mathilde smiled. It showed her in full, leaning slightly forward with an absorbed expression, glass in hand. The artist had saved himself the trouble of drawing her features by hiding her face behind her curtain of hair.

"If it's all right with you," said David, "I'd like to keep it as a souvenir. Fancy another drink?"

"Why did you go via a lawyer?" asked Mathilde, studying her glass, "You could have used a more direct method."

"I'll explain why, dear Mathilde, but then it's your turn to talk about yourself."

"I'll try."

"OK, I'll turn the clock back. When I realised I did want to meet you, I wondered how to contact you without giving the impression I was forcing your hand. As I had initially reacted badly to your mother's revelation, I felt you might do the same. Then I remembered the house I had impulsively bought for next to nothing just before I left France. Gifting it to you seemed the ideal solution. Because of my experience in the art world I know a bit about French law. I came over to Aix when the university broke up for the summer. Once there, I picked a lawyer's firm out of the directory at random and made an appointment. I was rather surprised the next day to meet a tall guy who looked nothing like a lawyer in a gloomy office under the eaves."

"Mr Olivier d'Estrello!" cried Mathilde.

"Exactly. It was a bit surreal. I thought briefly of giving up my idea and I think he sensed it. He's a perceptive person. His calm approach decided me, however. We started discussing the formalities, but the conversation quickly switched to Cézanne. We discovered our shared passion. It was June and it was hot. The secretary brought us refreshments. Time flew by. He had other appointments lined up, but he cancelled them one after the other. Finally we returned to the subject of the dossier. I asked him to play a discreet and rather ambiguous role. He must first 'bait' you, then bring up the issue of your origins while remaining vague about my intentions, to gauge your reaction without trying to influence you."

"He played his role to perfection."

"He's a model of discretion, I saw that at once. Chance is a wonderful thing."

"Sometimes."

Mathilde didn't know whether to laugh or cry.

Father and daughter spent the afternoon at the Orsay museum admiring Cézanne's paintings.

"I never come to Paris without visiting Orsay – it's like a pilgrimage. I presume you know that Cézanne painted Mont Sainte-Victoire from every angle. Most of his works are in museums abroad – in the States, Russia or in Japan where he has become a cult figure. Aix failed to recognise his genius while he was alive and France let most of his works leave the country."

They stood facing the one painting of Mont Sainte-Victoire that existed in the museum.

"I forgot to tell you a story about the house," said David suddenly, with a smile. "Your mother was convinced that Cézanne had been there to paint the mountain. I thought it was possible, nothing more, but she wouldn't back down. I teased her when she started prowling round the property looking for clues, perhaps even hoping to find a hidden painting. When I saw the owner to pay the first month's rent, I offered to buy the farmhouse. I had trouble understanding his *provençal* accent, but he said something like '*what would you do with it young man? It's just a pile of stones.*' The next month I tried again. At first he pretended not to hear me, then muttered into his moustache: *'You're after a Cézanne, is that it? I know you, Americans. Forget it, it's not worth your trouble, I've searched high and low'*. My response came like an inspiration: *'I'm interested in this pile of stones because it's where a wonderful love affair has taken place'* to which the old man said *'Consider it sold!'."*

He turned to Mathilde who had started to cry and drew her into his arms.

"I'm happy to pass it on to you. I hope that you will be as happy there as I was".

He gently drew back and gazed into Mathilde's tear-filled eyes. She was in a turmoil of emotions, unable to utter a word.

"I'm very proud to have such a lovely well-balanced girl for a daughter. We have missed out on quite a few years but we can make up for that, can't we?"

Mathilde nodded.

That evening they planned to have dinner on a *Bateau Mouche*. Olivier was to be the surprise guest. But spotting the lawyer on the jetty David merely feigned surprise:

"But I thought the case was closed!"

"There are a few formalities to be dealt with," grinned Olivier.

David turned to his daughter who was nonchalantly gazing out at the Eiffel tower.

"I see," he smiled.

As the boat passed the *Ile de la Cité*, Olivier couldn't resist reaching across the table to take Mathilde's hand. David rose to his feet with a glass of champagne:

"May I propose a toast to the beauty of my daughter, and to her health and happiness. Or should I say your shared happiness..."

Olivier in turn got to his feet. "Sit down!" hissed a furious diner, his photo of *Notre- Dame* spoilt.

Mathilde giggled into her napkin then started crying, as was her habit.

After dinner they accompanied David back to his hotel. He had to do a valuation in London the next day and was due to fly back to the States shortly after. He gave Mathilde a long hug.

"You are welcome to come and see us in Washington whenever you want. My family is keen to meet you. And Olivier, of course. By the way, my son John is studying law, in the hope of becoming a barrister. And Sarah is studying French literature, hoping to become a writer. You'd like her, Mathilde."

He shook Olivier's hand: "Look after my daughter."

"You can count on me."

Mathilde embraced him fondly.

They hailed a taxi.

"Avenue Trudaine" she said to the driver.

Olivier looked surprised. When they went to see Benoît they had stayed at his hotel.

"It's time I showed you round MY property."

He gripped her hand tightly in response.

They raced up the stairs like a pair of naughty children.

"It won't take long to show you round – there are only two rooms and no balcony."

She showed him the kitchen and the lounge. Olivier headed for the bookshelf and removed his glasses to examine the books. Mathilde laughed.

"Exploring the bookshelves is the first thing I do too when I go somewhere new!"

"Yours are better organised than mine."

"Really? Actually, I've just tidied the shelves."

She put on a CD.

"Would you care to dance, sir?"

"Mattie, you know perfectly well I can't dance. I'll step on your toes!"

"On my big feet you mean!"

"Ha ha!"

The opening bars of *Dancing Queen* came on.

"Come here, I'll show you. I could put you in touch with a professional dancer I know called Hubert who could teach you!"

They managed a few clumsy steps, then Olivier picked Mathilde up in his arms.

"Where's your bedroom?"

"Over there."

He put her down and paused in the doorway.

"Aren't you going in?" she asked.

"You're scared of snakes and scorpions and I'm scared of ghosts."

"There are no ghosts in this room, darling. Come in!"

She took his hand and pulled him towards the bed, removed his glasses and started on his clothes.

"Anyway, even if I once believed in them, I don't now."

He took her in his arms and laid her down on the bed.

CHAPTER 16

High above Mont Sainte-Victoire

Mathilde's long holiday at the *Bastide de l'Ange* was coming to an end. In those short weeks Olivier had shown her all round his property and opened up his heart. Their newfound love blossomed in the idyllic setting. She also witnessed duller days when the Mistral (a wind reputed to turn people mad) swept through the area or when rainstorms battered the house, gouging out ravines in the neighbouring fields and hills. But the bad weather never lasted long and was quickly replaced by clear sky, purer than ever.

Together they explored all the paths in the area, often stopping to admire Cézanne's landscapes so beloved to Olivier. Often Mathilde told herself that her mother, over thirty years before, must have felt the same emotions as she walked with David.

It was the last day before her return to Paris. She knew that back at her desk, Benoît would no longer be there to gaze at her lovingly. She was aware that from now on she would have go it alone and that worried her.

Olivier had organised their last hike in great detail but kept it shrouded in mystery. The weather was gorgeous and the sky its usual glorious azure blue. They had set off early up the slope to the top of *Mont Sainte-Victoire,* heading for the *Pic des Mouches* summit via the *Col des Portes.*

"It's a nice challenging trek" Olivier had announced, "Nothing your long legs can't cope with, darling. It won't be any more strenuous than climbing the *Rue des Martyrs* or the steps to Montmartre."

Mathilde started to tire only towards the end when the track become very steep and slippery. Olivier strode ahead whistling, only helping her past the tricky bits. Her legs felt leaden, her boots hurt her feet and her cap was giving her a headache. She was dying of thirst but Olivier ignored her pleas. "We can drink once we're up there," he promised. *Up there looks miles away*. She thought she would never make it. She lagged behind. Keeping her balance on the steep track by clutching a prickly bush, she paused. Some hikers with heavy backpacks skirted round her. She was near tears and at one point felt like turning back. But the idea of climbing back down the steep stony path terrified her.

Olivier's voice rang out across the mountainside:

"Mathilde! Mathilde! – I'm waiting for you!"

She looked up and saw his tall figure waving wildly.

"Keep going, don't be afraid. You're almost there."

She let go of the bush and scrambled upwards. Near the summit she grabbed Olivier's outstretched hands and he hauled her up.

"Well done Mattie!" he said showering her with kisses, "I knew you'd make it! Now, open your eyes and you'll get your reward."

The *provençal* landscape stretched out before them in all its wild rugged beauty and spectacular colours. Olivier pointed out the various mountain ranges and villages nestling in the valleys. With his binoculars she could even spot her house and the faint outline of the fig tree. She was so entranced she didn't notice that the walkers who had passed her were unfolding a parachute at the edge of the cliff. She gave an exclamation of surprise. Olivier grinned and challenged her.

"All set for a tandem flight over *Mont Sainte-Victoire*?" he announced.

"No way. I'm too scared!"

"Me too darling, but not for the same reasons. Come on!"

Gulping, she took his outstretched hand. They were both duly strapped onto the paraglider.

"Ready? You have to run without stopping to the edge of the cliff."

Mathilde took a deep breath: "I'm ready."

He pressed against her: "I love you, my brave little darling. Ready, steady...go!"

Hand in hand they took a running jump. The ground fell away beneath them. Mathilde closed her eyes tight. Olivier operated the parachute from behind and they soared into the air. Suddenly she felt a sense of elation and exhilaration, her fear gone. Nothing more could happen to her – they were welded together, conjoined.

The moment of ecstasy seemed to last forever. Then into her ear Olivier whispered:

"Mathilde darling, would you join your life to mine?"

She turned to look at him.

"Yes" she mouthed.

"What was that? The wind is making too much noise..."

"I said YES!" she yelled.

He handed her the ropes: "Your turn now."

"You're mad. I don't know how to steer."

Olivier put his hands on top of hers.

"Is it better if we do it together?"

"Yes please!"

"We're going to fly over the *Bastide de l'Ange*. Do you see the house?"

She managed to say yes.

"And the olive grove?"

"Yes, I can see it."

"There's a man walking through it – a tall man, a bit too tall. He's holding a little boy's hand. Can you see them?"

"Not yet."

"Have a good look. The man has put the boy's hand on the tree trunk, he's explaining something to him. The boy is listening attentively. His name is Jules."

"Jules is a rather old-fashioned name."

"It was my grandfather's."

"It'll come back into fashion one day."

He gave her a grateful kiss from behind.

"Ready to land?"

They touched down gently not far from the fig tree on her own property.

They both rolled across the ground laughing:

"That was the most awesome experience!"

"We can do it again whenever you want."

Tangled up in the paraglider lines they kissed passionately.

CHAPTER 17

The Bride's Bouquet

At the *Bastide de l'Ange* preparations were under way for the wedding celebrations in the warm month of October. Olivier and Mathilde had decided on a simple private wedding, although their friends and family still meant a considerable number of guests. The Stevenson clan had flown in from the States two days earlier. Friends from Paris turned up in dribs and drabs, and Olivier's parents, who had welcomed this surprise fiancée from Paris with open arms, gracefully and skilfully worked to put everyone at ease.

That morning Léa, Julie and Claire had arrived from the station by taxi. When Mathilde came out to greet them, she recognised the taxi driver from her first visit to the *Bastide* three months earlier. He asked if he could kiss the future bride.

"So the Parisian has fallen for our beautiful Provence!" he joked, "I knew that would happen! I wish you every happiness, *Mademoiselle.* Master d'Estrello is a good sort. I told you so, didn't I?!"

Before joining the procession to the village church, the guests were served refreshments prepared by Hortense. Over a glass of homemade lemonade, Micheline told David all about their daughter's childhood. Both were clearly moved but tried not to dwell too much on the past.

In dreadful English, Benoît discussed French literature with Sarah.

Hubert looked on amused as Frédéric attempted to flirt with Francesca who appeared to welcome his advances, thrusting out her bosom and laughing uproariously.

"I'm awfully sorry to leave you but I have to fetch my brother," said Frédéric "I'm his witness and he needs me around. Don't move, *bellissima*, I'll be back in a minute."

He rushed up the stairs to Olivier's bedroom and found him almost ready.

"So there you are! I need you to help me with these cuff links."

Frédéric obliged and said with a sigh: "I cannot believe you are getting married today. That's an exploit in itself but the fact it's Mathilde really gets me. The beautiful heiress whose dossier passed me by. I'll never get over it!"

He gave Olivier a friendly thump.

"You are bloody lucky, brother of mine. I must warn you that in my after-dinner speech I'll be relating all your amorous exploits. If Mathilde of the large feet doesn't ask for a divorce after hearing all that, I'll eat my hat!"

Olivier raised a clenched fist: "One more word out of you and I'll..."

"You can't disfigure me today of all days! There's this gorgeous woman downstairs. Italian. A real smasher. And a jet pilot to boot."

"You haven't forgotten the rings, have you?"

Frédéric patted his pocket.

"Are you ready?"

"Yes, let's go."

They embraced each other in true brotherly fashion.

"We mustn't be late" said Frédéric staunchly. Olivier noticed he had tears in his eyes.

In another bedroom along the corridor, the door firmly closed, Mathilde's three friends bustled around her. The bride wore a 1920's medium-length lace dress and a simple wreath of orange blossom in her hair. Her bouquet was composed of roses from the garden and sprigs from the olive tree.

"It's such a lovely idea!" breathed Julie.

"It's my homage to Olivier. Did you know that the olive tree symbolises wisdom, strength and fidelity? I think my Olivier is true to his name."

"When I think that three months ago you were really down and had given up believing in love," said Claire.

"Was it Hubert who revived your appetite for men?" asked Léa mischievously.

"Dear friends, that, I shall never tell you. It's our secret. But I admit that Hubert has played a considerable role in the whole romance."

"Time to go," announced Claire taking Mathilde by the hand. Mathilde reached out for Julie who in turn clutched Léa.

They descended in single file to find David waiting at the bottom of the stairs. When Mathilde reached the last step he opened his arms to embrace her.

"You look marvellous, my dear," he whispered into her ear, "I'm so proud and touched to be walking you down the aisle."

"Thank you *Daddy!*"

"I also wanted to say that you couldn't have found me a better son-in-law than Olivier."

Mathilde adjusted the white rose in her father's lapel and took his arm. A few hours before he had taken her aside to present her with his wedding gift. It was the portrait he had made of her mother at the *Mas du Figuier*.

"I've never been able to part with it, and today I'm so glad I kept it. I know it's not a Cézanne but its rightful place is here with you."

Mathilde, easily moved to tears, shed a few more.

On leaving the church on Olivier's arm she tossed the wedding bouquet into the crowd of guests, as is customary. It landed in Benoît's arms. Blushing, he handed it to Julie. The bride blew them a kiss then whispered something to her husband who responded with a smile.

The party was in full swing on the lantern lit terrace when Olivier whisked his wife away unnoticed by the guests. He took her to the Volvo concealed outside the grounds.

"Where are you taking me, husband of mine?"

"You'll soon guess..."

After driving a few kilometres through the countryside she realised:

"The *Mas du Figuier*!"

She laid her head on his shoulder.

"I'm so happy you thought of it."

"Our wedding night has been in my mind all day," he replied mischievously.

They left the car in the same place as that first time and used a powerful torch to light their way. Once past the trees they paused. Mathilde looked up at the countless stars glittering in the balmy night.

At the farmhouse door he picked her up and carried her across the threshold.

"Welcome to your new home," he laughed.

"OUR new home, sir!"

Inside the fire was ready to light in the hearth, food was laid out on the table and warm rugs lay invitingly over the chairs.

Mathilde raised her eyebrows inquiringly.

"I know, I had to break into private property but I was sure I wouldn't get caught. And now we're all set to survive a siege..."

She took his hand and drew him into the bedroom. He had to bend almost double to get through the doorway.

CHAPTER 18

A Family Photo

Five years later, at the Bastide de l'Ange

The house slowly awoke from the torpor of a hot June afternoon. A little boy played on the terrace, watched over by two women sitting in wicker chairs in the shade of the trellis.

A motorbike was heard coming along the drive, and then the doorbell sounded.

"Just stay there," said Mathilde to Hortense, "It's the photographer from *La Provence* newspaper. I'll let him in."

She went along the tiled corridor to the porch and saw Philippe removing his helmet. He gave her a kiss.

"Hi there, Mattie. How are you? What heat!"

"Come into the shade then. Olivier is in his office. I'll go and get him."

"Jules, come and say hello!" cried Hortense.

"Jules – that's a nice name," said Philippe to the boy.

"It's my dad's grandfather's name."

"How old are you?"

The child counted on his fingers: "Nearly four and a half."

"Well, well – you are tall for your age!"

"He's obviously taken after his father," laughed Hortense.

"And his mother."

Mathilde reappeared on the terrace.

"Olivier will be with you in a minute," she said to Philippe, "Take a seat."

She poured him a large glass of lemonade and turned to Hortense.

"Philippe has come here to take photos for an article about the launch of the *Huile d'olive de Provence* label which Olivier had been campaigning for alongside other olive growers."

"A family photo might be nice," said Philippe. "After all, the *Bastide de l'Ange* is an old family property."

"Good idea, but without me. It might be a bit awkward, seeing as I'm one of the Editors."

"True, I hadn't thought of that."

"There he is! Olivier, this is Philippe. He'd like to take a photo of you with your son."

"In the olive grove if possible" the photographer added, "The light is perfect at this time of day."

"As you wish. I always respect professional advice," said the Master of the House putting his arm round Mathilde and kissing her on the cheek, "Coming Jules?"

"Wait!" cried Mathilde.

Tenderly, she removed his glasses.

"But now I can't see!' he protested weakly.

"Your son will guide you along the path. I'll pop them into your pocket. You can put them back on after the photo shoot."

"It's all ready, just say when," announced the photographer.

"You know what," piped up Jules, "Soon we're going to plant an olive tree for my little sister. When we get to the field I'll show you the one my daddy planted for me. It's already quite tall."

"Marie has woken up from her nap," said Hortense, "I hear her grizzling. I'll go and get her."

"Stay where you are - I'll go," said Mathilde.

"But you're leaving me with nothing to do! You all spoil me rotten!"

"Don't worry – you are more than useful with your wonderful cuisine. Plus, I'm entitled to enjoy my daughter when I'm not working."

The housekeeper softened: "The apricot tart is cooling in the oven. I'll bring it out once they've finished."

"Good idea!" called Mathilde as she walked to the house.

Once in the bedroom she picked up her baby and went to the window. She opened the shutters, painted by Olivier in their original bluish grey, a perfect match for the pale pink ochre of the walls.

"Look, Marie, who's that down there? Can you see them? It's your daddy and your big brother."

Mathilde stayed for a moment at the window watching the men in her life. They were walking hand in hand towards the olive grove with the same supple gait. Marie snuggled into her mother's neck and Mathilde covered her little head with kisses. When father and son had disappeared under the olive trees she left the room.

"Let's go, my little darling. We'll wait for them with Hortense. They won't be long."

Slowly she walked down the stairs, along the corridor and into the summer glare.

***

Last word

I hope you have enjoyed this romantic escapade to Paris and Provence.

Stay in touch with my work through:

Facebook:

https://www.facebook.com/marielerougeromanciere

Instagram:

https://www.instagram.com/marielerougeromanciere/

I would be delighted to read any comments about this novel.

To contact me: marielerougeromanciere@gmail.com